POPULAR REWARDS

Maddie's
Magic Bicycle

and other stories

Award Publications Limited

*With thanks to Jill Atkins, Elizabeth Dale,
Marjorie-Ann Gladman, Jenny Jinks
and Lizzie Strong*

ISBN 978-1-78270-348-8

First published 2023

Published by Award Publications Limited,
The Old Riding School, Welbeck,
Worksop, S80 3LR

 /awardpublications @award.books @award_books
www.awardpublications.co.uk

23-1053 1

Printed in China

Contents

A Most Peculiar Present..................................5

The Snow Storm 25

India's Adventure 36

The Mystery of the Missing Frost.............46

Maddie's Magic Bicycle...............................62

The Lodger 73

The Naughty Knight....................................92

Panic on the Riverbank 108

Seagull Strife..119

The Lonely Bullfrog..................................136

The Magic Sprout 148

Grandpa's Gloves......................................159

A Most Peculiar Present

Olivia woke with a smile on her face. She'd been dreaming about her birthday all night and now the big day was here! And it was the school holidays so she could have fun all day. She only hoped Boots was there to share it with her…

She jumped out of bed and ran downstairs. Her mum, as always, was already in the kitchen and by the delicious smell, Olivia knew just what she was doing.

"Hello, darling! Happy birthday!" her mum said, giving Olivia a big hug. "Perfect timing, I've just finished cooking the first pancake for your birthday breakfast. Here you go!"

"Brilliant! Thanks, Mum," said Olivia, but then she glanced down at Boots's food bowl and her smile faded. It was still full.

"Boots didn't come back last night?" she asked.

"I'm afraid not," said her mum, frowning.

"After you'd gone to bed, your dad went out searching all over for her, but there was no sign of her."

"But that means we haven't seen her for a whole day! She'll be starving!" Olivia cried.

"Oh, knowing Boots she'll have got someone else to feed her," said Mum.

"But she might not! She never stays out this long, Mum. She might be stuck somewhere. She might be ill or…" Olivia's voice trembled. "She might have been hit by a car…"

"Dad drove around the streets last night, darling. You know Boots doesn't go far. If she'd been hit by a car, we'd have found her."

"Well, she has to be somewhere," said Olivia, grabbing her coat. "I'm going out to look for her."

"Have your pancakes first, darling," said her mum, "then you'll have more energy and Sam can join in, too, when he's up. It will be better if all we all look together."

"And Dad, too," said Olivia. "Where is he?"

"He had to go to work early."

Olivia stared at her mum. "On my birthday? He's gone to work without wishing me happy birthday?"

"He didn't want to wake you, darling. You were fast asleep."

"But he normally goes in later on my birthday, not earlier! We always have my birthday breakfast together."

"I know, darling. I'm afraid it couldn't be helped. He asked me to give you a hug and said you can open some presents without him. Here, have your pancake." Her mum slid it onto a plate. "Do you want bananas and cream on top?"

"I'm not hungry!" said Olivia, folding her arms.

Just then Sam walked in. "If Olivia isn't hungry, I'll have that pancake!" he grinned.

"No, you won't!" said Olivia. "We're going out to look for Boots."

"But—" Sam began to protest.

"Mum said we'd go once you were up," said Olivia.

"I also said we should eat first," Mum reminded her. "Let Sam have his pancake."

"Well, *I'll* have it if I've got to sit and wait!" snapped Olivia, grabbing the plate.

7

"I'm not sure you deserve it, talking like that," said her mum.

"I'm sorry," said Olivia. She knew she was being grumpy, but she was cross that her dad wasn't there to share her birthday breakfast, and she was worried about Boots.

They just had one pancake each and then they all went out to search for their beloved cat.

"Boots! Boots! Where are you?" Olivia called, as she walked down their garden path, but there was no answering miaow and no beautiful black cat came running to meet her. They went through the gate and hurried down both sides of the road, looking in gardens, calling her name. Then they went to the park, where Olivia carefully looked in all the trees to see if Boots was stuck up one, but there was no sign of her anywhere.

Finally, they gave up looking. "Maybe we should stick some posters on lamp posts asking if anyone has seen her," Olivia suggested as they reached home.

"We could put one up at the corner shop," said Sam.

"Good idea," said their mum. "Now then, I think it's time for another birthday pancake, don't you?"

"I'd rather make our posters first," said Olivia.

"I agree!" said Sam. He was as worried about Boots as Olivia was.

Olivia felt a lot happier once the notices were made and posted all round the neighbourhood. Mrs Bello at the pharmacy promised she'd mention Boots to all her customers, and the young man at the corner shop even photocopied some spares for Olivia. "She's such a lovely cat, I'm sure someone will have taken her in and be taking care of her," he said.

Olivia hoped so.

"Oh, and happy birthday, Olivia!" he called as they left.

"Thank you!" Olivia smiled. She'd almost forgotten!

"So, what would you like to do now, Olivia?" her mum asked after they'd finally finished their pancakes.

"Open my present!" said Sam, handing her a big parcel wrapped in yellow paper.

"No, it won't seem right to open presents without Dad here," Olivia said.

"Oh, you do have a gift from Great Uncle Eustace," smiled her mum. "It came in the post last week, and I hid it away so it would be a surprise."

Great Uncle Eustace wasn't actually part of their family. He was Olivia's godfather and a friend of Olivia's grandma. He travelled the world and always gave Olivia the most unique and amazing presents. Last year, she'd had a robot that did just what you told it to do, and the year before he'd given her a wind-up scooter. She'd been so looking forward to finding out what this year's gift would be.

A Most Peculiar Present

"I suppose I could open just that one," said Olivia excitedly.

Her mum passed her a small, thin package. Olivia tried to hide her disappointment.

"That doesn't look much!" said Sam.

"But the best presents can come in the smallest parcels!" said their mum.

Olivia hoped so. She took it from her mum and tore off the brown paper. Inside, her present was wrapped in shiny, silver paper.

"There's nothing there!" Sam laughed.

"Yes, there is," said Olivia. She could feel something hard. Maybe it was a magic wand?

With trembling fingers she pulled off the silver paper to find a note wrapped around... a pencil. Olivia stared at it, speechless. It didn't even have a coloured lead. It was just a boring, plain, pencil.

"What does the note say?" asked mum.

Olivia grew more hopeful as she unrolled the note. Maybe it was the start of a treasure trail to her real birthday present?

It wasn't. Olivia stared miserably at the spidery writing.

"To help in all your lessons. Enjoy!" Sam

read over Olivia's shoulder. "Oh, great, Olivia! Great Uncle Eustace has given you a pencil. Aren't you just so *lucky*?" he laughed. "And look, it's got an eraser on the end for all the mistakes you'll make!" Sometimes, her older brother could be a real pain, thought Olivia.

She frowned. She didn't understand. Why had Great Uncle Eustace done this? He went everywhere and came across all kinds of amazing things. She'd been hoping for something really wonderful. Why hadn't he sent her something more exciting than a pencil?

"It's a lovely present," their mum insisted. "It's very kind of Great Uncle Eustace to send you a gift."

Olivia glared at Sam and smiled a weak smile at her mother, then skulked up to her room in a foul mood. Dad wasn't here for her birthday, Boots was missing and now this big disappointment from Great Uncle Eustace. This was hardly the wonderful birthday she'd been looking forward to!

She flopped down on her bed and picked up the beautiful, sparkly notebook her friend, Izzy, had given her yesterday. She'd unwrapped it at the time and told Izzy how much she loved it. And she did. It had unicorns on every page. She would write her best stories in it.

Then Olivia picked up her diary and opened it. Yesterday, she had written: '*It's my birthday tomorrow. I can't wait to open my presents, especially the one from Great Uncle Eustace.*' Huh! She grabbed her pencil and started writing for today: '*Well, Great Uncle Eustace gave me this pencil and it's r...*' She was going to write 'rubbish' but somehow she found herself writing 'really great'. She stared at the words. What? How had that happened? Well, at least she could use the eraser on the end. But as she rubbed at the last words, they wouldn't disappear; they didn't even fade, no matter how hard she tried. What a *useless* present!

Angrily she wrote '*This eraser is r...*' but somehow she wrote '*really great, too*!' Olivia was really cross now! The stupid pencil seemed to be controlling her words. Well, not anymore! She'd show it who was boss. And

she snapped it in half! Olivia smiled spitefully. Unfortunately, just at that moment, her mum walked in.

"Olivia!" she cried. "What are you doing?"

"It's a stupid, nasty pencil!" she cried, flinging the pieces on the floor. "I don't want it! I wish Great Uncle Eustace had never given it to me."

"I really can't believe how ungrateful you are, Olivia!" Mum replied. "Your great uncle doesn't *have* to give you anything. He went to the trouble of buying it, wrapping it up and posting it to you. I think you should use it to write a thank-you note to him. Now!"

Olivia stared at her mum, gobsmacked.

"Write a thank-you note! On my birthday!" she cried. "No way. That's not fair."

"That's enough, Olivia. Do as you're told."

Olivia folded her arms. "No!"

"Pardon?"

"It won't write what I want it to!"

"Don't be silly," said her mum. "You can stay in your room until you've written your letter."

"You don't understand…!"

"I understand that you are behaving like a spoiled brat and you need to sit and think about how ungrateful you're being!"

"But—"

"Enough!" her mum thundered. "I don't want to hear any more."

Olivia couldn't believe it. Her birthday had just got a thousand times worse. It was so unfair! That pencil was so nasty, changing her words. And her mum wouldn't even listen.

Sam came and poked his head around her bedroom door.

"What have you done?" he asked.

"Nothing!"

"Oh, it's so bad you can't tell me about it?" he grinned.

Olivia just glared at him, scared that if she spoke, she might burst into tears.

"Ignore me, then!" he said. "But I want you to know you're ruining my day, too. I thought we'd be having fun on your birthday, but you're spoiling everything."

Olivia frowned as he closed the door. He was right. She could spend her birthday sitting in her room or she could apologise and write the thank-you letter. It would only take a few minutes and then she could finally start to have some birthday fun.

A short while later, Mum called Olivia downstairs.

"I'm sorry, Mum," said Olivia. And she genuinely was. "It's just... nothing's going right for me today."

"Well, let's see if we can change all that," said her mum, hugging her. "Write your letter and then it's done."

Olivia ran back upstairs. She frowned. Her

bedroom door was open. She was sure she'd closed it behind her. She burst inside. Oh, no! Her new notebook lay open and the first page had scrawly writing on it. Sam! Sam had been in her room and spoiled her new notebook! And her pencil lay beside it. He'd used it. She wouldn't even be able to rub it out!

"Sam!" she yelled. "How could you?"

He peered around the door. "What?" he asked innocently.

"You've ruined my new notebook! I hate you!"

"What on earth's the matter now?" asked their mum, coming in.

"It's Sam! I was saving my new notebook for my best stories, and he's scribbled all over it!" cried Olivia.

"That was very naughty of you, Sam," said their mum. "But I think you're making a bit of a fuss, Olivia. It's only in pencil; you can rub it out."

"I can't!" she cried, flinging the pencil on the floor again. "The eraser doesn't work! It's stupid!"

Her mum folded her arms sternly. "Not

again, Olivia!" she said. "I'm very disappointed in you. I don't want to hear another word from you until you've written a *nice* letter to Great Uncle Eustace – with the pencil he sent you."

Olivia slumped onto her bed. This was the worst birthday ever. She burst into tears.

Sam tiptoed in. "I'm sorry," he said. "Please don't cry, Liv. Mum's right. It will rub out."

"No, it won't! I told you!"

"Let me try," said Sam. And he picked up the pencil and started rubbing at the words. Then he stopped. "Wait, I didn't write this!" he said.

"Oh, Sam!" Olivia said. "Of course you did!"

"I didn't!" he said. "I wrote the first words, *'Olivia is really angry with this gift and I'm not surprised.'* But I didn't write the rest. Honestly! Why would I? Look, the handwriting is different."

For the first time, Olivia looked properly at the writing on the page. The words read *'Olivia is really angry with this gift and I'm not surprised. She doesn't understand that it doesn't write what she wants it to write, it writes what she needs to know.'* She frowned.

Sam didn't fool her. He'd simply changed his writing.

"Liar!" she snapped. "Go away!"

As he walked out, she tore the page out of her notebook. It was then she noticed the pencil. It was no longer snapped in two, but whole again, like new! Olivia should have been confused, curious or even a little scared, as she knew full well that she had snapped the pencil in half. But she was too cross now and she snatched up the pencil and wrote under Sam's words *'I am having the most awful day.'*

But, strangely, even though she'd finished, the pencil carried on writing. Try as she might, she couldn't stop it. This was crazy! She stared at the words it formed. They read, *'but it will be good in the end.'* How could this awful day possibly turn into a good one now? Too many bad things had already happened. Her dad had gone to work early, her mum was horribly cross with her, Boots was lost, her notebook was ruined and she had to write this silly thank-you letter for something she didn't even want. Not only did this stupid pencil have a mind of its own, but it told lies. Crossly she

wrote *'Sam is being horrible'* and once more
the pencil insisted on writing more words. She
frowned as it added *'because he is jealous that
Great Uncle Eustace doesn't send fab presents
to him.'*

Suddenly Olivia stopped. She'd never
thought about that before. Poor Sam. How
ungrateful she must seem. Especially now
that what seemed to her to be such a dull
gift had turned out to be something truly
extraordinary.

She carried on writing. *'I'm sad that Dad
went off to work without wishing me happy
birthday or having breakfast with me.'* But
once more the pencil carried on writing. *'So he
could come home early for a surprise birthday
trip.'*

What? Olivia gasped. She couldn't believe
it! If the pencil was right, they were going
somewhere special and that's why her dad
had gone early! He *did* care about her. He'd
left early to make her birthday extra special!
She was thrilled and horrified. She'd been so
horrible and selfish all morning.

What a brilliant pencil Great Uncle Eustace

had given her! It seemed it really was telling her everything she needed to know.

Just then, Olivia thought of something she needed to know more than anything else.

'*Boots is...*' she wrote. And her pencil continued: '*stuck in the shed next door with her six kittens.*'

"Kittens?" cried Olivia and she jumped up, raced downstairs, and ran into the corner of the garden by next-door's shed.

"Olivia!" her mum shouted after her. "Did I tell you that you could come down...?"

"Shh, Mum!" Olivia put her finger to her lips. Something about the look on her face made her mum approach her quietly. They both stood still and then they heard it. The faintest mewing.

"Boots!" Olivia whispered. "She's in the shed!"

"Oh, well done! Let's get Sam and go and fetch her."

Fortunately, their neighbour was in and she quickly took them out to the shed. As she unlocked the door, the mewing grew more frantic, and when the door opened, they all

gasped. There was Boots, surrounded by six beautiful kittens, just as Olivia's magic pencil had said. "Oh, Boots! Thank goodness we've found you!" cried Olivia, picking her up.

"We didn't even know you were expecting kittens!" cried Mum.

They carefully carried them all home and made a lovely warm bed for them in the kitchen. Once they were settled, Boots ate all the food in her dish.

"She was starving, poor thing!" said Mum. "Thank goodness you found her, Olivia!"

Olivia smiled and thought, *Thank goodness for Great Uncle Eustace's magic pencil!*

"Whoops!" she said. "I have to write that thank-you letter!"

"Well, don't be long!" said Mum. "We're going out soon."

"Where are we going?" Sam asked.

But as she ran up the stairs, Olivia heard a car door slam and she peered out of her bedroom window and smiled. It was her dad! He'd come home early after all! Her bad birthday was turning good, just as her magic pencil had said it would. And all thanks to it telling her what she needed to know. Oh, it was going to be so useful!

'Thank you, Great Uncle Eustace,' she began writing. And her pencil carried on, *'you have given me the most brilliant present ever!'*

Olivia laughed. It was right!

The Snow Storm

Chase and Logan were always glued to their computer. They loved to play racing games, fighting games, adventure games – anything they could get their hands on. They would play from the moment they got up in the morning right up until bedtime, if their dad would let them.

When their cousin Ryan got the brand new Super-X console for his birthday, Chase and Logan couldn't wait to visit him and try it out. And finally their dad had arranged to take them to their aunt and uncle's house for the weekend.

"It's meant to have surround sound, so you feel like you're actually *in* the game!" said Chase as they packed their bags ready to go.

"Kit, at school, said the controls even vibrate, like when you come off the track on the racing games and stuff!" said Logan.

The two boys could barely sleep that night,

they were so excited. When they woke up the next morning, they hurriedly dressed and took their bags downstairs. They wanted to get going as soon as possible. Their dad was already up, having a coffee at the kitchen table and listening to the radio.

"Come on, Dad, drink up. We want to get going!" Logan said, dumping his bag by the door and slipping his feet into his shoes ready.

"Hang on, boys, haven't you two looked outside?"

Chase and Logan looked at each other, and then out of the window. The garden was blanketed in thick, white snow, and large flakes were still flurrying down.

"Wow, it hasn't snowed like this in ages!" gasped Chase. "I wonder if it will be snowing at Ryan's house."

"I'm afraid it is. The snowstorm has affected pretty much the whole country," Dad told them, taking another sip of steaming coffee.

"Never mind," said Chase. "We'll just wrap up extra warm. I'll get the hats and gloves."

Chase was about to run out of the room when his dad stopped him.

The Snow Storm

"Hang on, Chase," he said with a grave look on his face. "The weather is much too bad for us to go anywhere. They're saying on the radio that all of the major roads have been closed. I'm sorry boys, but it looks like we're snowed in for the weekend."

"Snowed in?" Logan said in disbelief. "But we can't be, we're supposed to be going to Ryan's to play on the new Super-X console. We *have* to go."

But their dad wouldn't budge.

"It's much too dangerous to travel today.

We'll just have to go another weekend."

Logan and Chase slumped down onto the sofa. It was so unfair. Their weekend was ruined, all because of a little bit of snow.

But it wasn't just a little bit of snow. The storm continued, and the snow piled deep outside. Not that the boys had any idea. Once they had got over the shock of their ruined weekend, they quickly cheered themselves up with a computer game. An hour later they had forgotten about the snow entirely. That was until the screen went black and their computer turned off.

"What's going on?" Chase said, switching the on and off button a couple of times, but nothing happened. "I think it's broken. I'll get Dad."

When Chase found his dad he was flicking light switches.

"Looks like the storm has caused the power to go out," he said, tutting as he tried the switch one last time.

"No power?" Chase said in alarm. "But how will we play our computer games?"

His dad laughed. "You're just going to have

to find something else to do."

"Like what?" said Chase sceptically. "There's nothing to do around here without the TV or computer. This is the worst weekend ever!"

"Why don't you take Buster for a walk in the park?" Dad suggested, handing Chase his lead. "You could all use a little exercise, and you can enjoy being out in the snow. It'll be fun!"

Chase and Logan trudged miserably through the deep snow while Buster bounded happily ahead of them, jumping into huge snowdrifts and barking at the falling snowflakes. The boys thought there was absolutely nothing fun about snow at all. It was cold and it was wet. What was fun about that?

As they walked through a coppice of trees, a heap of snow fell off a branch above Chase and landed on his head. Logan laughed.

"Hey!" Chase said, grabbing a handful of snow and throwing it at Logan.

"What was that for?" Logan dusted the snow splatter from his coat.

"For laughing at me," said Chase, shaking

the remaining snow from his hat as Logan grabbed a handful and threw it at Chase in retaliation.

The boys ran around throwing snowballs back and forth, laughing as they hit each other – laughing harder when they missed! Meanwhile, Buster jumped around madly trying to catch the flying balls in his mouth.

Chase began to roll a huge snowball, pushing it through the snow to build it up. But it became so big that he couldn't lift it.

"Let's turn it into a snowman," Logan suggested, rolling another, smaller, snowball to make the head. They used branches for its arms and Logan put his hat on its head. They didn't have a carrot for its nose so Chase found a stone instead.

Buster barked up at it.

"All right, we'll make a snow dog, too, Buster," Chase promised, and the boys got to work moulding more snow into the shape of a small dog with a little stick for a tail. "It looks just like you, Buster!" Chase laughed. Buster yapped happily, bouncing around his new snow dog friend.

The boys flopped down on the ground next to their snowman, exhausted.

"Hey look, I'm a snow angel!" Logan said, lying back and waving his arms and legs backwards and forwards through the snow. Chase began to do the same, and Buster rolled around making his own dog angels.

But then the boys started to shiver. They were very wet and getting really cold. Deciding it was time to head back home, they said goodbye to the snowman and snow dog and jogged home, shivering. But when they arrived, they found that the house wasn't much warmer.

"I think the pipes have frozen, the heating won't work," their dad explained. "But I've lit a fire so it will heat up soon. Then maybe we can have a snack."

The boys liked the sound of that.

The fire crackled and burned, and soon the boys had warmed up and dried off. Their dad managed to heat some water over the fire and make them all a delicious hot chocolate. They snuggled their cups to warm themselves. Chase and Logan dunked biscuits into their drinks and gobbled them greedily – playing in the snow was hard work! They were both starting to think that maybe a snow day wasn't so bad after all. But once they had finished their snacks both boys began to feel bored again, and all they wanted to do was go back to playing their computer games.

"Why don't we play a board game instead?" Dad suggested. The boys didn't look thrilled. They hadn't played a board game since they were little, but they were pretty sure they were boring and babyish.

Dad came back a few moments later with a dusty stack of old board games he had dug out from the back of a cupboard. With nothing else to do, the boys shrugged and agreed to play. And before long they were actually enjoying themselves. They played every game in the pile, and Logan was very pleased that he won every one. Chase pretended that he thought the games were stupid, but it was only because he hadn't done very well. Secretly, he had really enjoyed them.

After the games were finished it was getting dark, so Dad lit some candles. They made

spooky shadows up the walls.

"That gives me an idea," Dad said. He put his hands together and made a strange shape, but on the wall the shadow looked just like a rabbit.

"Wow, that's cool! How did you do that?" Chase asked. So their dad taught them how to make all sorts of shadow creatures, from rabbits, to eagles, to reindeer. And then he told them a spooky ghost story, using the shadows to act it out. The boys sat in silence, completely engrossed in the performance. Suddenly the lights pinged back on. The boys jumped in surprise.

"The power's back!" Dad said, smiling. "I guess you boys will want to go back to your computer now, won't you?"

"Actually," Chase said, "we'd really like to know how the story ends."

So they turned all the lights back off and spent the rest of the evening telling ghost stories and making shadow puppets by candlelight.

"I'm sorry it wasn't the fun weekend you were hoping for," said Dad when he tucked them into bed that night.

"That's OK," Logan said. "In the end, I think it turned out even better."

India's Adventure

Oscar's toy elephant, India, was snuggled up on his pillow, the same way she had been every night since he was a baby. India had gone everywhere with Oscar when he was little. But now Oscar was older and had started school, India couldn't go everywhere with him.

After years of cuddles, India's fur was no longer soft and smooth. She'd long ago lost one of her button eyes, and one ear dangled loosely. But her tiny silver bell around her neck still shone as bright and tinkled as merrily as the first day Oscar had met her. She loved Oscar very much and she knew he loved her, too.

It was Saturday, so Oscar didn't have to rush off to school and leave her today.

There was a shout from downstairs. "Are you awake, Oscar?" It was his mum. "Time to get up. Grandad's here."

India knew how much Oscar loved his

grandad. They always had such fun together.

Oscar grabbed India and ran downstairs.

"Hello, Oscar! Hello, India," Grandad greeted them.

India noticed that Grandad was carrying a large bag. She wondered what was inside.

"Here you are, my boy," said Grandad, holding the bag open.

Oscar leaned forward and peered inside and lifted out a football.

"Thanks, Grandad. Can we go to the park to play with it?"

"In your pyjamas?" laughed Grandad.

Oscar laughed. "Won't be a minute!" He sped upstairs and was dressed in double-quick time. Then he gobbled his breakfast and put on his coat. Pushing India into the top of his backpack, he tugged it over his shoulders.

"Ready," he said.

India felt rather uncomfortable. Oscar had been in such a hurry, he had shoved her in upside down and, as he trotted along beside Grandad, she was bumped up and down, up and down until the most dreadful thing happened – India fell out of the backpack!

"Help!" she called, but Oscar didn't hear.

India landed on the edge of the pavement and rolled down a grassy slope. Feeling bruised and dizzy, she lay still, waiting for Oscar to come back for her. But he didn't come.

It was cold and damp in the ditch where she had landed. Surely Oscar would miss her soon and come looking for her. But as time passed, India's worries grew. What if Oscar didn't miss her? Was his new football more important? She'd heard other toys talk of children growing too old to have a cuddly toy.

It was time she moved. She planned to climb up the slope so that Oscar would see her on his way home. She stood up and began to plod towards the path but she tripped on her tatty ear and slid back down to the slope. She tried a second time, but the same thing happened. Her ear was just too loose, and it dangled down almost to the ground.

"Oh, dear, what am I going to do?" she sighed.

Then, as she glanced up, she noticed a beautiful spider's web dangling between two branches of a small tree. The web was covered in dew that sparkled like stars. In the middle of the web sat a spider.

"Hello, Spider," called India. "Your web is beautiful. You're so clever to spin such a wonderful web."

The spider swung down on her long, silken thread and landed beside India.

"Thank you," said the spider. "That's kind of you to say. You've made me very happy." The spider came a little nearer. "Would you like me to sew your ear back on? I couldn't help noticing that it needs mending."

"Oh yes, please," said India.

So the spider found a pine needle and sewed India's ear with her shining silver thread. India smiled. Her ear felt great, and she flapped it happily.

"Thank you," she said as the spider climbed back up to her web. "That's much better. Now perhaps I can climb that steep slope and my ear won't get in the way."

But she slid back down once again.

"Oscar," she called. "I'm here! Please come and find me!"

But Oscar didn't come and India began to fear the worst – maybe Oscar *had* grown too old for his cuddly elephant. Maybe he didn't need her anymore.

India couldn't help the tears that fell as she slumped down at the bottom of the slope, feeling very sorry for herself.

Suddenly, something black-and-white fell clumsily down and landed in heap of feathers in front of her. India stepped back, startled.

It was a magpie with a piece of string caught in its wing. He stood up and pecked at his wing, but could not pull the string out.

India's Adventure

"Poor you," said India. "That looks very uncomfortable. Let me help you."

India used her trunk to untangle the string and, with a final tug, she pulled it free.

The magpie flapped his wings. "That's done the trick!" he said. "Thank you so much. Nobody has ever helped me before. You've made me very happy." He tucked his wings into his sides. "Would you like me to find you a new eye? I couldn't help noticing you only have one."

"Oh, yes please," said India. "But where will you find one?"

"I collect shiny things," said the magpie. "I'm sure I have a button somewhere in my hoard." And off he flew.

While India waited, she thought about Oscar again. Even if she had a mended ear and a new eye, she still didn't know how she would get back to him. And even if she did, would he still want her?

When the magpie returned, he was carrying a shiny blue button in his beak.

"What a pretty button," said India.

At that moment, the spider came sliding

down her silk thread once more. She sewed the button in place for India, and stood back to admire her work.

"That looks marvellous!" said the magpie.

"It feels marvellous, too," India laughed. "I can see so much better now. Thank you so much!"

Then, all of a sudden, India's laughter bubbled away.

"Oh dear," said the magpie. "Don't you like your new eye, after all?"

"I love it," said India. "But I still don't know how to get back to Oscar."

India told the magpie all about her life with Oscar, and how she had fallen from his backpack and down the slope.

"How will I ever get back to him?" asked India.

The magpie looked at her with his head on one side, deep in thought.

"I know!" said India, remembering the magpie's love of shiny things. "If you could carry me home, I would gladly give you my silver bell!"

"What a brilliant idea," said the magpie.

"Why didn't I think of that?"

Up and up he flew until he was above the treetops with India dangling below him.

India was so excited. She was on her way home!

Soon, she saw Oscar's house below them. The magpie swooped down and landed on the window ledge outside Oscar's bedroom.

"Thank you, Magpie!" said India. She pulled the silver bell from around her neck and gave it to the bird.

"You're welcome," he replied, "and thank *you*!" He took off, ringing the little bell as he went.

India waved to the magpie until he disappeared from sight, then she peered into Oscar's room. Oscar was sitting on his bed looking very sad. Just then, he looked up and saw her.

"India!" he yelled. He leaped up and ran to the window. He flung the window open and grabbed her, hugging her tightly.

"I've been searching everywhere for you," he said. "I thought I'd lost you forever."

Then he held her in front of him and stared.

"You look fantastic," he laughed. "Someone must have mended you, although I see you lost your bell. But how did you get up on the windowsill?"

India knew Oscar would never know the secret of her adventure, but she felt so happy and was sure he did, too.

The Mystery
of the Missing Frost

It was autumn, and Mother Nature and all her fairies were busy getting everything ready for the changing of the season. They sprinkled their magic over the trees, turning the leaves from green to gold to fiery red. They tucked the flowers back into their comfy beds before the harsh, cold bite of winter hit. They helped the animals to make their nests and get their burrows and holes ready for a long sleep through the coming cold months. It was a busy time of year for the fairies. Everything had to be ready before Jack Frost arrived.

Jack Frost was King of Winter. The other fairies thought he was a cold, rude sprite. They wished that they could just skip winter and go straight to spring. But Mother Nature told the fairies that every being had a place and a use on Earth, including Jack Frost. The fairies knew that without his winter making all the animals and plants take a rest and refresh themselves, there could be no spring; no new life. So the fairies put up with Jack, but they avoided him as much as they could – especially on the days when he seemed particularly frosty. Instead, when winter arrived, they busied themselves with preparations for the Yule Ball: a huge celebration held by all the fairy folk at the end of each year. It was one of the most exciting events in the fairy calendar.

The time had come for autumn to draw to a close, but there was no sign of Jack Frost. The weather stayed unseasonably warm. Summer birds stayed and enjoyed the warm weather. Even the flowers continued to grow new blooms as if it were still summer! The whole land was in confusion.

The fairies dashed about here and there trying to convince the animals that it really *was* time to settle down, but none of them paid any attention. The days went on and on and still Jack – and winter – was nowhere to be seen.

"Where is he?" asked Pix, a little tree fairy. "He's normally here by now. Winter is going to be late!"

"Or not at all!" flapped Twinkle, a young flower fairy who always worried about everything.

"Oh, you know Jack," said one of the older fairies. "He's probably off causing trouble somewhere he isn't wanted."

Time ticked on and still Jack Frost did not come. The woodland creatures were getting very tired, sleepily dragging their feet. Some of them, like the hedgehogs, should have been tucked up and hibernating a long time ago, but it was much too warm outside for them to settle. The plants were looking very sorry for themselves, too, unable to hold their heads up to the weak sunshine that shone down.

The fairies knew things couldn't continue this way, but they didn't know what to do about it. They would have to ask Mother Nature for advice, but no one was willing to disturb her. She was very busy and important, and should never be disturbed except in an *absolute* emergency.

"I'll go," Pix volunteered bravely. He had never met Mother Nature before, but he was sure she would be kind and helpful and sort out this mess for them.

Pix flew to Mother Nature's tree house in the middle of the forest. He had heard people talk about how beautiful it was, but nothing could have prepared him for what he saw.

The tree was huge – at least four times wider than all the other trees – and its branches twisted and stretched high up to the sky. Every animal and plant imaginable was featured on its bark like a beautiful mural, intertwining and winding around the trunk and up into the branches. It seemed to shimmer and sparkle as though it were infused with magic.

Pix stared up at the tree, mesmerised. He looked for a door but there didn't seem to be

one, so he knocked on the trunk of the tree and hoped someone would answer.

"Yes?" The voice seemed to come from everywhere.

"Mother Nature?" Pix quivered nervously. "I'm sorry to disturb you, but Jack Frost hasn't come. There is no winter, it's still autumn. All the creatures and plants are so very tired. What should we do?"

"Well, it seems you must find Jack Frost," said the voice.

"But how?" asked Pix.

"You must find a place where winter never rests!" The glow of the tree dimmed, and Pix knew he wouldn't learn any more.

Mother Nature hadn't helped him at all. How was he supposed to find Jack Frost? He didn't know *any* place where winter never rested. What did that even mean?

When he got home, Twinkle was waiting for him.

"What did Mother Nature say? Is she going to fetch Jack Frost?" she asked, her eyes wide with worry.

"No," said Pix.

"Then what are we going to do?"

"He might be miserable and rude, and maybe nobody likes him, but the fact is we *need* him. And if no one else is bothered about finding him, then I'm going to find him myself... somehow," Pix said. He knew without even asking that none of the other fairies would help him. They didn't care about Jack. They thought the world was better off without him.

"You can't go by yourself!" said Twinkle. She paused, and then in a voice barely louder than a whisper said, "I'll come with you."

Pix looked at Twinkle. She was the most nervous fairy he had ever met. But he wasn't going to turn down the offer of company because he *really* didn't like the idea of facing Jack Frost alone. "Thanks, Twinkle."

"So, where are we going?" Twinkle asked.

"Well, the thing is... I don't actually know," Pix admitted. "Mother Nature told me I'd find him where winter never rests. But there isn't anywhere like that."

"I think I know!" Twinkle squeaked excitedly. "There's a place I've heard some of the elves talk about," she said in a rush of words. "It's right in the middle of the Dark Forest, called the Ice Lake, where the forest is so thick that the sun can't get through. It's so dark and cold there, that the lake is frozen all year round, even in the summer!"

"That could be the place Mother Nature was talking about. Brilliant, Twinkle," said Pix and Twinkle blushed. "Come on, there's no time to lose. Let's go and find Jack!"

When they reached the Dark Forest, they could barely see through the first line of trees, the shadows were so dark and deep. Both Pix and Twinkle hesitated, neither of them sure they wanted to go into the forest after all. But Pix knew that Mother Nature would be counting on him, so he stepped bravely into the shadows with Twinkle hurrying nervously along behind him.

The forest was too dense for the fairies to fly, so they stumbled along on foot through the tangle of tree roots until their eyes adjusted to the darkness. They hoped they were heading in the right direction. It seemed to be getting colder, and they began to shiver.

Finally, they spotted something glistening ahead of them. Pix ran towards it. It was the frozen Ice Lake, large and blue, and glowing as if there were lights beneath the ice.

"It really does exist!" Twinkle gasped.

"But where's Jack?" Pix asked, looking around for any sign of him. "He must be here somewhere."

There was certainly a lot of frost everywhere. The whole area around the lake was crusted in a thick layer of sparkling white. They were sure he must be here somewhere.

Then Twinkle pointed to a tuft of frozen grass. There, so pale he almost blended into the frost he created, sat Jack Frost.

"Jack! Jack!" Pix called out, shaking the sprite by the shoulder. Jack's skin was cold and hard. He didn't stir.

"Do you think he's OK?" asked Twinkle, peering worriedly at Jack's still figure. "You don't suppose he's… you know?" She quivered at the thought.

"I'm fine," said an icy voice. "Leave me alone."

"Jack, it's time for winter! You need to come," Pix reminded him.

"I don't *need* to do anything," Jack said coldly. "You think my job is so easy, sprinkling a bit of frost here and there, bringing snow and ice and the cold north wind all on my own while everyone else is off celebrating. Well let's see just how easy you all find it without me."

Pix didn't know what to say. He had thought Jack *liked* working alone.

"We can't do it without you, Jack," Twinkle said gently. "Nobody can bring in winter like you can. We need you."

The Mystery of the Missing Frost

To Pix's surprise, Jack seemed to soften a little at Twinkle's words.

"Nobody needs *me*," said Jack gloomily. "Nobody thinks of me at all. All anyone thinks I do is destroy things and make everything worse. Nobody wants to be around me. I don't even get invited to your stupid Yule Ball."

"Everyone is welcome. We didn't think you wanted to come!" said Pix, amazed. "You don't even seem to like any of us. You're always so... frosty."

"It would be nice to have been invited. To feel included," said Jack sadly. "I've always been separate from you lot. You all disappear when I arrive. It gets lonely seeing in the cold winter all on my own. And then for the rest of the year nobody wants me around. Who do I get to celebrate with? To have fun with? And then there's my job. You all get to do things like bringing flowers and light and colour to the world. Everybody loves you. Nothing I do gets appreciated. Nobody thinks *my* work is beautiful."

Jack sniffed. As he spoke, tiny, delicate snowflakes began to fall all around him, the air got a little chillier, and the sparkling frost spread its swirly icy fingers further into the forest around them.

Twinkle looked around at the frozen forest, and then at Jack, looking so unhappy. She had never thought before about how lonely he might be. No wonder he was so prickly and grumpy; she was sure she would be, too. She sat down next to him and put her arm around him. She shivered a little from the cold, but she didn't pull away, and surprisingly, neither did Jack. No one had ever given him a hug before. It felt warm and nice.

"I think your work is beautiful," said Twinkle. "These snowflakes are so delicate, and each one is different. And look at the swirly patterns in the frozen lake. It's like a beautiful painting. I love seeing the sparkle of frost on the grass in the morning, like it's been sprinkled with glitter."

Jack seemed to thaw a little as he listened to Twinkle.

"And think about how much people love the winter. Crisp morning walks, building snowmen, sledging. Ice patterns on their windows. You bring so much joy to all the children," Twinkle went on. "We all need you, Jack. Don't give up. Come back with us. Come to the Yule Ball. I want you there. Please, Jack. It's not too late to change your mind."

Jack turned his face away.

"Come on, Twinkle," Pix said. "We can't make him come with us if he doesn't want to."

Pix started walking away. Twinkle gave one last look back at Jack, who still had his face turned away. A pile of snow was building up around him where the snowflakes were settling. Maybe Pix was right. They were going to have to find a way to make do without winter this year.

Later that night, while all the fairy folk were tucked up in bed, Jack crept out of the forest to take a look at the world. He walked through the moonlit park where the flowers drooped, looking tired and sad. He slipped down a street where unused sleds lay abandoned in sheds.

He saw a light on in a bedroom window and a little boy peering out. Jack jumped up to listen as the boy's mother came in.

"What are you doing?" the mother asked.

"Waiting for it to snow," the boy said, excitement gleaming in his eyes. "It *will* come, won't it? It always snows in winter."

Jack walked on through the quiet streets thinking about all he had seen. Maybe the world did need him after all.

The next morning, Twinkle awoke with a start. Someone was banging on her door loudly.

"Twinkle, Twinkle, come and see! He did it! He came back!" called Pix.

Twinkle jumped out of bed and threw open the door. Everything had been painted a brilliant frosty white overnight. Jack was back! Twinkle laughed with joy. She knew he wouldn't let them down.

All the fairy folk were excited that winter had at last arrived and they could finally have their Yule Ball. Preparations began for it that very day. All anyone could talk about was Jack Frost, wondering why he had decided to return, and where he had been. Twinkle kept an eye out for him all day. She hoped he might still be around somewhere so that she could thank him. But wherever he was, Jack was keeping well out of sight.

Finally, it was time for the Yule Ball. It was held in the middle of the big meadow at the edge of the wood, which had been transformed into a winter wonderland. It was decorated from top to bottom in beautiful paper snowflakes. Everything glistened icy blue and snowy white. It looked magical. All the fairies, elves and pixies wore their best clothes and came together to celebrate the end of the year.

Twinkle still watched hopefully for Jack. Finally, she saw a pale face standing in the shadows at the edge of the meadow.

"You came!" she said, rushing over to him.

Jack looked around the meadow in disbelief.

"It's all decorated like... well, like me!" he said in amazement.

"Of course it is. This is a celebration of winter!" Pix said. "This party is all about *you*!"

Jack couldn't believe it. All this time he had kept to himself, thinking everybody hated him and hated winter. But here they were celebrating it. And just like that, Jack relaxed, and even managed a smile.

The Mystery of the Missing Frost

Twinkle and Pix took him round to meet everyone. Once they got to know him, folk realised Jack wasn't grumpy and rude at all. In fact, they were surprised at how shy he was.

It was good to see Jack enjoying himself, so Twinkle and Pix were surprised when they saw him sneaking away before the party was even halfway through.

"Jack!" they called. "What's wrong? Aren't you having a nice time?"

"I've had the best night of my life," Jack said truthfully.

"Then why are you leaving?" Pix asked.

"Because it's nighttime, and I've got a job to do," Jack replied with a twinkle in his eye, and he slid out into the shadows.

Pix and Twinkle watched him go, dancing happily around the branches of the trees and across the grass. Wherever he went, he left a sprinkling of sparkling frost behind him. It was winter at last, and everywhere was beautiful.

Maddie's Magic Bicycle

Maddie was very shy, so she was happiest when she was on her own. Sometimes, she played with her big brother, James, but if his friends came to the house, she ran upstairs and hid in her room. Now that she was used to her teacher, she liked going to school, but she preferred to sit by herself. If someone spoke to her, she hunched her shoulders, closed her eyes and pretended she wasn't there.

"Would you like to bring a friend home from school?" Her mum asked one day when she met her at home time.

Maddie shook her head.

"It's your birthday next Sunday," said Mum. "You could invite some friends to your party."

"I haven't got any friends," Maddie muttered with a sigh. "And I don't want a party."

The following Sunday, Uncle Dave came

for lunch. Maddie liked Uncle Dave because he was funny. She didn't feel shy with him because she had known him all her life.

"I've brought you a birthday surprise," he said as soon as he arrived. "It's outside."

Maddie followed Uncle Dave out to his car. He opened the boot. Inside was a beautiful, purple and green bicycle.

"Wow!" said Maddie. "Thank you!"

Uncle Dave nodded. "It's a magic bike," he said as he lifted it out of the boot.

"Magic?" gasped Maddie, unsure. "But I don't know how to ride a bike. I might fall off."

"I'll teach you," said Uncle Dave. "And you won't fall off. I told you, it's magic. The magic will help."

They wheeled the bike onto the pavement and Maddie balanced on the saddle. She could *just* reach the pedals.

"These are magic trainer wheels," said Uncle Dave, pointing at the two little wheels on either side of the back wheels. "They'll stop you falling off."

Uncle Dave was right – it was magic. Maddie didn't fall off, and riding the bike felt good.

They raced up and down the path, with Maddie pedalling and Uncle Dave running beside her. After a while, Maddie saw two children from her class walking towards her, but she was too nervous to speak to them. She didn't know what to say. So she kept her head down and rode past. But she did manage to smile.

A short while later, Mum called Maddie and Uncle Dave in for lunch, but as soon as they had finished eating they went outside again.

"You're so good at this, I'm going to take the trainer wheels off," said Uncle Dave.

"But I'll wobble and fall off," Maddie complained.

"No you won't," said Uncle Dave.

They sped up and down the path again, with Uncle Dave holding the back of the saddle. Then suddenly, Maddie realised that he wasn't beside her anymore. She started to wobble.

"Don't forget the magic!" called Uncle Dave.

Maddie gripped the handlebars and kept going... and she didn't fall off.

"That's clever!" called Mrs White, the lady next door, as Maddie came to a stop outside

her house. "What a beautiful bicycle!"

Maddie smiled. "Thank you," she said. Then she gulped and felt herself go red. That was the first time she had ever spoken to Mrs White.

On Monday, when Maddie came out of school, there was Mum, holding her new bike by the handlebars.

"I like your bike," said Amy, a girl in her class.

Maddie smiled. "Thank you, I got it for my birthday," she said. She was just about to tell Amy it was a magic bike when she suddenly realised she had spoken. She jumped on her bike and pedalled swiftly away, feeling hot and embarrassed again.

Maddie and Mum went to the park. There

were loads of children there. Some were on bikes, some were on the swings, others were running around. Maddie stopped when she saw them. She was sure they were all staring at her.

"I want to go home," she said.

But then the bike seemed to twitch and its colours glowed brightly. It seemed to be saying, "You're OK, Maddie. Just hold on to me and off we'll go."

Bravely, she rode around the park until it was time to go home.

The next day, her gran came to visit.

"I've got a new bike, Gran. It's magic!" said Maddie.

"I'd love to see you ride it," said Gran.

So off they went down the road, with Maddie riding ahead and Gran strolling along behind.

Suddenly, a ball rolled out through a gateway right in front of Maddie. She swerved and almost fell off, but the magic bike straightened up just in time. Maddie stopped and picked up the ball as a boy ran out from his front garden.

"Sorry," he said.

"That's OK," said Maddie. "My magic bike saved me."

"Magic? That's cool!" said the boy.

Maddie threw the ball to him and he ran back the way he had come. Maddie couldn't believe it! She had spoken to the boy. The bike's magic must be very strong.

Just then, Gran caught up.

"Time to go back now," she said. "You ride really brilliantly."

Maddie felt really good as she pedalled home.

On Wednesday, Dad needed to go to the shops, so Maddie went with him – on her bike of course. As they arrived, Maddie saw old Mr Philpot who lived in the flats opposite Maddie's house. He waved to her and, instead of turning shyly away as she usually did, Maddie waved back. She wobbled, but the magic bike didn't tip over.

"Keep both hands on the handlebars," Dad said.

"But I was waving to Mr Philpot," said Maddie with a smile.

"That's nice," said Dad. "You've never

waved to him before, have you?"

Maddie shook her head and grinned.

"It must be your magic bike," laughed Dad.

On Thursday, Mum and Maddie went to watch James play football. Maddie took her bike and rode it round and round a small track not far from the football pitch. She'd not been there long when Amy and Jacob from her class arrived. They were riding their bikes, too.

"Hello, Maddie," said Amy as they all stopped side by side. "Is your brother playing in the match?"

Maddie nodded and smiled. She liked Amy.

"So is mine," said Jacob. "He's the one with the pony tail."

Maddie looked at Jacob. He was OK, too.

"I'll race you both to the grass at the end of the track!" said Amy.

"One… two… three… go!" shouted Jacob.

At first, Amy was in the lead then Jacob caught her up. Maddie pedalled as hard as she could.

"Come on, magic bike," she whispered. "We can do it!"

In the end, they all reached the grass

together.

"A dead heat!" Jacob laughed. "That's some bike you've got there, Maddie."

"Thanks. I got it for my birthday," said Maddie as they began to ride back to the start.

On Friday evening, James said he wanted to go to the skatepark where there were ramps to ride bikes.

"Why don't you come, too? You could bring your bike," Dad said to Maddie.

Maddie thought about it. She knew there were always crowds of children at the skatepark on a Friday evening and the ramps looked quite scary. Then she thought about her bike. It was magic, after all, so maybe it would be fun to try.

When they reached the park, Dad and Maddie stood beside the ramps and watched the other children as they swooped and jumped and spun. It looked really exciting, but Maddie didn't know if she would dare try it. She slipped her hand into Dad's as James zoomed by on his skateboard and leapt into the air.

"Hello, Maddie," said a voice behind her.

It was Jacob, with Bertie and Annabelle who were also from her class.

Only last week, Maddie would have backed away or hidden behind Dad, but now she smiled at them. "Hello," she said.

"That looks scary," said Bertie.

Maddie nodded.

"Are you going to have a go, Maddie?" asked Annabelle.

Maddie looked at her bike. It was glowing brightly in the sunshine. Was it trying to persuade her to go on the ramps?

"I will, if you will," she answered.

"OK, let's all go!" grinned Jacob.

They wheeled their bikes onto the edge of the ramps. Then one by one, they rolled down the first slope and up the other side.

Maddie felt her tummy flip as she whooshed down the ramp.

"This is fun!" she shouted to Annabelle and they went again and again.

Maddie was tired but happy when she went to bed that night.

"Mum," she said, yawning, "is it too late to have a party?" Maddie asked. "Because now

Maddie's Magic Bicycle

I've got some friends I'd like to invite."

Mum was thrilled.

"I think my magic bike helped me to feel brave," said Maddie.

The following Saturday, Maddie had her belated birthday party. She invited Amy, Annabelle, Jacob and Bertie. They all brought their bikes so they could ride the ramps before coming back home for a very special birthday tea. And when Mum carried the cake into the room, Maddie had a big surprise. It was in the shape of… her magic bike, of course!

The Lodger

Delilah was a large, cuddly cat with silky, silver fur and sparkling green eyes. Today, like most days, she was snoozing on her special heated bed – a fleece cradle that hooked over the radiator and was always comfortably warm. "Oh, my life is so perfect," she purred.

"Hello, Delly Welly!" It was Tom, the young boy who lived in Delilah's house. "How are you, my gorgeous pussy cat?"

Delilah rolled onto her back, waiting for Tom to stroke her soft tummy. "I'm fine, thank you, my dear Tom," she said, although Tom could only hear meows. "You're right, I am gorgeous, but please don't call me Delly or Welly."

After a while, Tom ran off to play in the garden and Delilah sat up and stretched. "This heated bed is just a bit too toasty," she said to herself. "I think I'll get a drink." She waddled into the kitchen and slurped some of her water. As usual, her food bowl was full up with delicious kibble. She ate some – even though she wasn't that hungry – then she pushed through her cat flap and stood on the patio.

"Ah!" She breathed in deeply as the breeze rustled her whiskers. "Nothing quite like fresh air."

After a few seconds, however, she turned round. "Right that's enough. Phew! I'm worn out!" And she headed back into the kitchen. As she trotted past her empty food bowl, she paused. "Now that's odd," she said. "I'm sure I didn't eat *all* of my food. Where's it gone?"

She wandered into the living room. "I guess I must have eaten it all without noticing! Silly me!" She crouched, ready to leap onto her bed, but then stopped and let out a high-pitched yowl.

There was another cat in her bed!

"*What?*" she spat. "Who are you?"

"Oh, hello," said the cat, calmly washing his ears. He was small and slender with ginger fur, a pink nose and long, elegant whiskers. "Hope you don't mind me popping in. I'm

Lionel, but call me Lino."

Delilah could feel her tail fluffing up to twice its normal size. "Yes I do mind, actually! That is *my* bed you're sitting in… and I suppose you ate my dinner, too!"

Lino licked his lips. "Gosh, yes, sorry about that, but I was absolutely starving. You see, my owners—"

"I don't care how hungry you were," interrupted Delilah, pacing up and down. "This is *my* house, *my* food and *my* bed." She prodded the warm cushion with her paw. "So clear off back to your own house."

At that moment, Tom burst into the room. "Oh, my gosh!" He rushed over to Lino. "It's a ginger cat! Isn't he beautiful?"

"Excuse me," said Delilah glaring at Tom. "I'm the one who's beautiful round here, remember?"

Tom ignored Delilah's grouchy meows and scooped Lino into his arms. "You're so adorable, and so tiny. Don't they feed you? And look at your eyes – perfect pale green – I love green eyes."

"Hello?" Delilah weaved in and out of Tom's

legs. "I've got green eyes too you know! "

But Tom wasn't listening. He cradled Lino as if he were a baby and carried him into the kitchen. "Would you like some food, little ginger cat?"

"No he wouldn't," shouted Delilah. "Because he's already eaten *everything*."

Tom poured more chicken-flavoured kibble into the bowl and watched as Lino scoffed the lot. Delilah stared in disgust. "That's two bowls he's eaten in the last five minutes! What a greedy pig!"

The kitchen door opened and Tom's dad poked his head round. "What's going on here?" Then he noticed Lino.

"At last," thought Delilah. "Someone to see sense and get rid of this furry trespasser!"

Tom stroked Lino's tail. "He was in Delly's bed, Dad. Please can we keep him?"

Dad's face softened. "He probably belongs to someone else. We can't just keep him."

"Exactly!" said Delilah. "Listen to your father, Tom."

"Hang on a minute," said Dad, looking more closely at the purring Lino. "I think I've seen him before. Yes, look, his name tag says 'Lino' and he lives two doors down from us at Bill's house."

"Hooray!" said Delilah. "Back to Bill's you go. Hurry up please."

Tom looked crestfallen, but Dad gently picked up Lino and carried him out of the front door. "I'll take him back and check he's definitely Bill's cat."

"Thank goodness for that," said Delilah, running up to Tom. "Now you can give me a proper cuddle."

But Tom was thinking about Lino and only absentmindedly tickled Delilah's ear before wandering off.

"Well, really!" Delilah shuffled back to her bed. "How rude. Don't expect me to sit on *your* lap later."

The next morning, Delilah was enjoying the fresh air in the garden once again. She sniffed a few plants, said hello to a blackbird (which flew away) and strolled casually back into her house.

"I think I'll take a little snooze on Tom's bed for a change," she said, climbing the stairs.

She reached Tom's room and took a running jump onto the bed. "AAAArgh!" Delilah jerked backwards, falling onto the carpet.

That cat! He was there. Ginger-Greedy-Guts himself, sprawled out on the duvet, muddy paw prints all over the pillowcase.

"Morning!" Lino stretched and yawned as if he'd been there all night. "I've been here all night! It's so brilliant here!"

Delilah flicked her tail. "Yes I know it's brilliant. It's *my* house. Who said you could sleep on this bed?"

The Lodger

Lino sat up. "Um… I didn't actually ask. I just popped through the cat flap and up the stairs."

"How *dare* you?" said Delilah, furious.

"Well, you didn't notice." Lino rested his nose on his paws. "You were fast asleep in your bed. *Snoring*."

Delilah was about to protest that she didn't snore, it was just a sinus problem, when Mum walked in. "Hello!" She stared at Lino. "Where did you come from?"

Tom came out of the bathroom. "Oh, Mum, please can we keep him? He's so lovely and look, Delilah loves him!"

"I do *not* love him!" hissed Delilah. She tried to stand on Tom's foot.

Mum sat on the bed and stroked Lino's ears. "Ooh, he is rather handsome, isn't he? "

"Pah!" said Delilah.

"But where's he come from?" said Mum. "We can't just take him."

"Oh, it's Bill's cat again!" said Dad. "I knocked on Bill's door last night, but there was no one home. I just had to leave the cat in the garden."

"Hmmm." Delilah glared at Lino. "He didn't stay in that garden very long, did he? Thought he'd break in here and eat all my food and sleep on all my beds... er... what are you doing, Tom?"

Tom had picked up Lino and was carrying him downstairs, singing to him. "Who wants some tasty treats? Who wants to live with us?"

Delilah charged after them. "This is outrageous!"

Things got worse throughout the day. Wherever Delilah went, Lino was there first. All her favourite places: the sunny patch in the hall; the pile of clean washing; the airing cupboard – not to mention her own, private radiator bed!

The final straw came when Delilah went for a light bite and found her bowl not only empty, but upside down with chunks of food scattered on the floor! "Is it not enough that he eats my food?" sobbed Delilah. "That he sleeps in all my best snuggly places? But he has to mess up my house too? This has got to stop!"

The next day, Delilah launched Step One of *Operation Get Rid of Lino*. She trotted down the garden to one of Dad's favourite flowerbeds and started digging in the wet mud with her front paws. Trying not to vomit, she picked a clump of earth up between her teeth. It was disgusting! Slowly, she carried the mud back to the house where she dropped it into her food bowl. It looked horrible, but Delilah was sure Lino wouldn't notice. He was such a guzzler.

Delighted with the first part of her plan, Delilah clambered onto the kitchen windowsill. From there, she could watch the ginger cat as he gobbled up breakfast and was given a muddy surprise! She settled down confidently to wait. It was beautifully sunny on the windowsill and Delilah soon fell asleep.

She woke some time later, her tummy rumbling with hunger. Without thinking, she climbed down, padded across the floor and buried her face in her food. After a few mouthfuls, however, Delilah started to think something was odd. Why did her kibble taste so strange? She took another bite and swallowed. "Perhaps Tom chose a different flavour – fish maybe, or… "

Delilah stopped chewing and stared, her eyes bulging, her mouth hanging open. "Oh, no!" She spat brown stuff over the floor tiles. "I've fallen for my own trap!"

The kitchen was filled with retching sounds as Delilah spluttered and coughed, spraying half-eaten mud and food across the room. "Save me!" she yowled running towards the back door. She stumbled through the cat flap and lay on the cold patio, gasping.

"Hello, Dels!" It was Lino, sauntering past on his way to the house. "You look a bit poorly today, if you don't mind me saying."

Delilah glared at him as he hopped through the cat flap, with a flick of his ginger tail.

"Would you look at that?" said Delilah,

bitterly. "He thinks he lives here!"

Step Two of *Operation Get Rid of Lino* was easier – Delilah hoped. It involved digging in the garden again, but Delilah was feeling confident. After yesterday's mishap, she was determined to get that pesky long-whiskered intruder out of her home. She padded over to the hedge just outside the back door and started to tug at a large piece of prickly twig.

"NGGGG!" She pulled with her teeth. "NGGGG!" She dug her claws into the earth, straining and panting. At last she managed to drag the twig onto the patio. It was very prickly indeed, but Delilah didn't let that bother her. Without pausing to rest, she squeezed through the cat flap and dropped the stick on the floor. Then she settled on the windowsill ready to watch the action.

It didn't take long. Within a few minutes, Delilah heard the familiar flapping sound of the cat flap and Lino's pink nose appeared, followed by his showy-offy long whiskers. There was an agonising pause while he sniffed the air, and Delilah worried he might not come in. But finally, his whole body slipped into view and... OUCH!

The little cat let out an ear-splitting yowl and the house erupted. Mum stormed into the room, bashing the door against the wall. Dad nearly tripped over his own feet as he galloped up from the garden and Tom actually trod on his mother.

"Sorry, Mum," said Tom, rushing to Lino, who was holding up a paw with the thorny twig stuck to it. "Look! There's a thorn in his paw! He's bleeding!" Tom lifted Lino into his arms and kissed the top of his head. "Poor pussy cat, look at your poorly paw!"

Delilah toppled off the windowsill and tried to climb into Tom's lap. "It's just a little scratch, he'll be fine. Stop fussing over him. He's attention-seeking!"

No one paid Delilah any attention. Mum opened and closed cupboard doors, searching for some antiseptic, while Dad carefully removed the twig and patted Lino's paw with a wet tissue. "Hold still, there," he said in his special *talking-to-a-cat* voice – the one he normally saved for Delilah. "Let's clean this up for you." He carried on dabbing and glanced at Tom. "Where did that bramble twig come from?"

Tom shook his head. "No idea… oh, Lino! Is he going to be OK?"

Delilah put her head on her paws. "Of course he'll be OK. What a ridiculous question." She wandered to the edge of the room and stared at her family. They seemed to love Lino even more now. "My plan has failed," she thought crossly. "I'll have to go outside while I think what to do next." And she plodded off to sit in the cold garden.

Hours passed and it was getting very chilly, but Delilah didn't want to go back in the house. Not while everyone cooed and oohed over that bothersome Lino. She stood up, pushed through a gap in the fence and kept on walking.

She squeezed through another gap and then another, before arriving in an unfamiliar garden. It was darker now and she wanted to go home, but she was still feeling sorry for herself. "Perhaps I can find a different family," she thought. "Like Lino did." She crept down the garden path, towards the house. It was the same shape and size as her home, but the windows were dark and it seemed very quiet.

As she reached the back door, Delilah heard someone meowing. She stopped walking and hid behind a potted plant. It was Lino! He was staring at the door, yowling. Delilah suddenly realised where she was. This was Bill's garden! Lino had come home!

She peered through the plant leaves and watched as Lino carried on crying. His whiskers and tail were shaking and he looked so small and scared. "Why doesn't he just go through his flap?" wondered Delilah. But then she noticed the back door had no flap! He couldn't get in!

"Lino?" she moved out of the shadows. "Why are you sitting here in the dark? The house is empty. Look there are no lights on."

Lino stopped meowing. "Yes I know, but Bill's usually back by the evening. It's a matter of waiting."

"Oh, I see," said Delilah. "How long do you have to wait?"

"Hours." Lino sat on the doorstep. "I keep calling in case he's forgotten me."

The Lodger

Delilah squinted at Lino's paw and a stab of shame hit her. "How's your foot? Does it really hurt?"

"It's not too bad, just a bit sore. I don't know where the prickly thing came from, but I should have been more careful."

Delilah was glad it was dark, because she could feel her ears going pink. Just then a light came on in the house and Lino started meowing again. The door flew open and Bill plonked a plate of food on the ground. Lino tried to push past him but Bill's foot kept him out. "No, Lino, sorry. You can't come in."

"What?" gasped Delilah. "How cruel!"

Lino nibbled his supper sadly while Delilah watched. "Do you ever go in the house?" she asked. "I mean, ever?"

Lino shook his head. "I used to, but everything's changed. Bill says I make him cough and itch. It's something called an allergy." He pointed at a rickety shed next to the house. "I sleep in there. It's got cushions and things, but it gets cold in the night."

Delilah peeped into the shed. The first thing she saw was a mass of cobwebs with

dozens of spiders staring back at her from the dark corners. She sniffed a cushion and her whiskers crinkled at the smell of damp and mould. She thought of Lino here, shivering and alone, and she let out a wail.

"OHHHH!" She fell onto the horrid cushions. "I can't bear it! I'm sorry, Lino!"

Lino's ears twitched in confusion. "What's the matter?"

"I tried to make you go, I tried to poison you, to injure you – I *did* injure you! And all along you were suffering… neglected! Abandoned!"

Lino stared at his feet, he didn't know what to say.

"Come home with me now!" Delilah stood up and went towards the door. "Come home, Lino. We'll share. You and me. I don't need all that space and all that food. Bill doesn't want you but Tom does. Oh, do come home. Please!"

Lino's ginger face lit up and his green eyes sparkled. "But I thought you hated me."

"I was just jealous," admitted Delilah. "I didn't know how lucky I was to have my wonderful family and my home and when I think of you out here in this mould-infested spidery shed…" Delilah shuddered.

The two cats purred and rubbed their heads together in a truce. They trotted back through the various gaps in the hedges, Delilah leading the way. "Tom's dad will check with Bill," she told Lino. "So he knows where you are. It will all work out. You'll see."

"I do hope so," said Lino as they neared home.

Before either of them could nudge the cat flap, Tom flung the door open.

"They're here!" he shouted. "Delilah! Lino! Oh, I was so worried!" He bundled both cats into his arms and carried them into the house.

Later, after a fresh helping of kibble, Delilah leaped neatly into her radiator bed and smiled at Lino. "Come on then," she said. "There's plenty of room for two."

Lino leaped in beside her and snuggled up to his new friend. Delilah closed her eyes and sighed happily. Poor Lino. No wonder he'd wanted to come into this house. Imagine being shut out all day and then forced to sleep in a cold shed! She felt ashamed of how she'd treated the little cat. Tom loved them both.

The Lodger

There was no need to feel jealous. Delilah felt the warmth of Lino curled next to her and realised how lovely it was to have a friend and to share. There was plenty of food and space for them both.

After a while, Lino lifted his head. "Thank you for letting me stay, Dels," he said, trying to stretch his legs out. "Do you mind if I ask you something?"

"Yes, of course, whatever you want."

Lino rested a paw on Delilah's leg. "Can you budge up a bit?"

The Naughty Knight

Norman was a trainee knight. He went to knight school where he learned things like how to sword fight, protect the kingdom, and rescue people from tall towers. But Norman was not a very good student. He didn't like listening to long, tiresome lessons. He got all twitchy and fidgety if he sat still for too long, and he found it so hard to concentrate on what his teachers were telling him. As far as he was concerned, Norman thought he would be much better riding his horse around, fighting off actual baddies and just getting on with being a knight. So while everyone else was busy learning and furiously scribbling down notes, Norman found himself messing around.

All day long, whenever the teacher turned his back, Norman would pull funny faces and play practical jokes on his classmates. He loved practical jokes. From slippery soap on the sword hilts so that they couldn't be held properly – he liked playing this trick on his friend, Arthur! – to sneezing powder and whoopee cushions, he drove all the other students crazy.

"Stop it, Norman!" his friends complained. "You'll never be a knight if you always misbehave." But Norman just couldn't help himself. He knew he would make a *great* knight, but he just couldn't take anything seriously.

When the day finally arrived for the knights' test, all the trainees gathered at the castle gates feeling excited and confident. Everyone, that is, except Norman. He was quite sure he could be an excellent knight. He felt as brave and as strong as any knight had ever been. But along with not being very good at lessons, he wasn't good at tests, either. Norman hung anxiously near the back of the group. What would he do if he didn't pass this important test? All he had ever wanted was to be a knight. It was all he thought about, all he dreamed about. Norman felt sick with worry as they all waited for the huge gates to be opened.

But the gates never did open.

"What's going on?" Donald huffed. He was the teachers' pet and a know-it-all, and Norman didn't like him very much. Norman didn't know why Donald should worry – everyone loved him. He came from a long line of knights, and Norman was sure that he would pass the test just by turning up and smiling at the teachers.

Finally, the king came out onto the balcony, and a hush fell over the waiting crowd.

"Attention, everyone!" the king cried. "Today's test has been cancelled."

"Oh, bother!" muttered Donald.

Yes! thought Norman.

"As some of you may have noticed, a dragon arrived in the kingdom last night and has been seen flying around the town," the king continued. "No one is safe until it has been removed. We will be calling on all of our knights for their assistance."

Norman felt a surge of hope. Maybe this could be his chance to prove how he could be a brilliant knight. He could finally get some real hands-on experience!

"None of you students should attempt to find the dragon and fight it yourselves," the king said very seriously. "You are not yet qualified to take on such a task. Please leave it to the professionals. A dragon is incredibly dangerous. All your tests will resume as soon as the dragon is gone. Don't worry, I'm sure it will only be a couple of days."

Just then a shadow passed over the top of the crowd. Screams and gasps echoed around the walls and the king ran back into his castle for cover. Norman looked up to see a huge, fearsome, fiery red dragon swooping overhead, with smoke streaming out of his its nostrils.

"Awesome!" gasped Norman. It was his first, real dragon!

Two days passed and the dragon was still there, causing chaos and destruction around the kingdom. Its mighty roar rumbled the mountains, sending rocks crashing down into the town below. It flew over regularly, burning the trees and crops to a crisp with its fiery breath. It even flew into the king's castle one day and stole all his treasure! No one was brave enough to stop it. The kingdom was a mess, and the people too terrified to even leave their homes.

Many brave knights went up the mountain in search of the cave where the huge beast had made his home. They were all confident that they could get rid of the dragon. But one by one they returned covered in scratches and bruises, with their hair singed, and too terrified to even speak. Since they all refused to go back, it seemed the dragon was there to stay.

"What can we do?" the townspeople cried as they gathered outside the king's castle demanding answers. "The kingdom is being destroyed. There's no one left to help us."

"It seems we have no choice," the king declared. "We will have to leave."

"Leave?" came the surprised mutters from the crowd. "But where will we go? What about our homes?"

Everyone was in a panic. They couldn't leave their homes, but they couldn't stay while the dragon destroyed everything.

Norman, however, was not listening. He

The Naughty Knight

was too busy thinking. He had a plan. A plan, he thought, that was just crazy enough to work. So, while everyone else went home to pack up their things ready to leave, Norman went home to pack his own bag.

That night, as everyone slept, Norman picked up his bag and crept quietly out of his house. He looked around the dark town, half destroyed by the terrible dragon. He took a deep breath before setting off down the long, winding road that led to the mountain, where an orange, fiery glow lit up a cave near the top.

It took Norman a long time to climb the steep path that wound up the mountainside. A low rumble and puffs of smoke swirled out of the cave above. The dragon was at home and fast asleep.

Norman finally reached the cave and poked his head inside to get a proper look at the beast. It was the first time Norman had ever seen a real dragon up close before, and what a sight it was! It was huge. *Enormous*. Far bigger than Norman had imagined. It was covered with shining red scales and it had long, sharp teeth that poked out of its mouth, and a spiny tail that curled right around its body. It looked incredibly fierce. What's more, Norman noticed that it was sleeping on top of a big mound of gold and treasure – more riches than he had ever seen in his life. His task was going to be even more dangerous than he had thought. Briefly, the idea of running back home to his nice, warm bed crossed his mind. But Norman knew he was the only one left who could possibly rid the kingdom of this dragon. He had come this far – there was no turning back now. He carefully tiptoed inside the cave, and bravely approached the sleeping dragon enjoying dreams of gold and treasure.

Not for long, thought Norman, as he undid his bag and got to work.

When he'd finished, Norman crept back out of the cave and crouched down behind a rock, just outside.

"This had better work," Norman whispered to himself as he reached into his bag for the last part of his plan. And then… *POP*! He exploded a huge party popper that he had made specially. The bang echoed loudly around the cave, while colourful paper streamers filled

the air and landed in a tangled mess all over the dragon, which woke with a terrible fright.

ROOOOOAAAAAAR! The beast leaped to its feet, banging its head on the roof of the cave, its wings all tangled up in the streamers. It landed on a pile of nettles that Norman had placed around it and, as it rolled around, roaring in pain from the stings, it sent clouds of blue powder into the air – sneezing powder that Norman had left all around the cave.

ACHOOOOOO! the dragon sneezed. *ACHOO! ACHOO! ACHOOOOOOOOOOO!*

The Naughty Knight

Huge plumes of smoke and flames shot out of the cave, lighting up the mountains for miles around. Norman couldn't resist looking inside to see what was happening. The dragon was rolling around on the floor as Norman's nettles drove it mad. All the while, its sneezes became stronger and more persistent. Huge gusts of hot air and flames continued to fill the cave, sending more clouds of the irritating powder up into the air. It was such an extraordinary sight that Norman had to stifle a giggle so he wouldn't be noticed. But just then, the dragon started squirming and wriggling towards the mouth of the cave, and Norman had to dart out of the way.

Once out of the cave, the dragon flapped its huge wings, breaking free of the streamers. Then it launched itself off the mountain and flew, far away from the kingdom, its fiery sneezes lighting up the night sky as it went. Norman watched it go until the last flashes of light faded beyond the horizon.

"Yes!" cried Norman, punching the air in triumph. "He won't be back any time soon." Norman was very pleased with himself. His plan had worked!

There was too much treasure for Norman to carry by himself, but he quickly gathered up as much as he could and stuffed it into his backpack. Then he scampered back down the mountainside to the sleeping town below.

The next morning, Norman was so tired from his nighttime adventure that he overslept. His mother came in and opened the curtains, letting sunlight stream through the window.

"Wake up, Norman!" she told him, shaking him by the shoulders. "Get up! It's gone! The dragon has gone! We're saved! We're all saved! Come on, Norman, get up!"

Norman's mother bustled back out of the room again, leaving him lying in bed. A smile spread across his face. The night before felt like a dream, but when Norman reached under the bed his fingers found his backpack, still bulging full of treasure. It had all been real! He had done it!

As the news spread that someone had managed the impossible task of ridding the town of the fearsome dragon, the townspeople began to fill the town square, amazed and excited.

Finally, the king came out onto the balcony once more. A hush fell over the crowd.

"I am pleased to tell you that the dragon has gone!" declared the king. "The kingdom is safe!"

An almighty cheer rose up from the crowd and echoed around the mountains. "Whoever managed this impossible task must surely be the bravest knight the kingdom has ever seen, and they will be greatly rewarded. Please come forward, brave knight, so that we can give you the thanks that you deserve."

The townspeople looked around at one another, waiting to find out whom this brave person might be.

Norman slowly pushed his way forward through the crowd.

"Norman, come back!" hissed his mum. "What are you doing?"

But Norman continued towards the king.

"Excuse me, Your Majesty," Norman called up to him.

The king looked down at Norman, who

seemed very small and unimportant.

"Not now, young man," the king said, irritably, looking back out into the crowd. "We are trying to find our hero."

"But, Your Majesty, it was *me*," Norman said. "*I* got rid of the dragon."

"You?" said the king with a slight chuckle. "Don't be ridiculous. Only someone really strong and brave could have done such a thing."

"But I did, Your Majesty. I went up there last night while everyone was asleep. I can prove it."

Norman pulled the heavy backpack off his shoulder and opened it, revealing all the sparkling, golden treasure. The crowd gasped. The king's jaw dropped and a very serious and stern expression grew on his face.

"Who are you, boy, and where did you get that?" the king demanded.

"I'm Norman, sir. I went up to the dragon's cave last night and used all of my best practical jokes to drive the dragon crazy, and it flew away. It won't be back in a hurry!" Norman said, grinning at the memory. The king was staring at him. Norman couldn't decide if he looked surprised or angry.

"Norman?" said the king slowly. "Ah, yes, I've heard about you. You're one of our trainee knights, aren't you? Have a fondness for messing about in class, I hear. Hmmmmm."

Norman stared down at his feet, his cheeks burning. How did the king know that? He couldn't believe he might be in trouble again, when he had only been trying to help.

The king's fingers twitched on the hilt of his sword, and Norman flinched, sure that he was about to be punished.

"Well, Norman. It's not exactly how I expected the job to be done, but you have managed to succeed when all my other knights failed. You know you were told not to go looking for that dragon, don't you? Terribly dangerous. But then you never have been one for rules... You remind me a bit of myself when I was your age."

He drew his sword out of its scabbard. Norman fell to the ground, preparing for the worst, but then the sword gently tapped his shoulder. Norman risked looking up at the king, who had a twinkle in his eye and a smile on his face.

Touching the sword to Norman's other shoulder, the king proclaimed, "Arise, Sir Norman, a true knight if ever there was one."

Norman stood up, hardly able to believe what had just happened.

"Now then, you'll need a knightly name. Let me see…" The king thought for a moment, then, "Ah! Of course! Three cheers for Sir Norman the Joker!"

The crowd broke into cheers and applause, and Norman stood speechless, a huge grin on his face. This was the best moment of his life, made even better when he saw Donald's disbelieving face staring back at him from the crowd.

"Sir Norman has found all my treasure," the king said happily. "There is enough here to help rebuild our kingdom. And with the dragon gone, we can all stay!"

"Hurrah!" cheered the crowd again.

The whole kingdom was in the mood to celebrate. After the biggest party ever seen, they all worked tirelessly together to rebuild

the kingdom until it was even better than before.

Norman found being a real knight better – and harder – than he had ever imagined. The dragon never did return to the kingdom, but they knew that if it did, Sir Norman the Joker would be waiting.

Panic on the Riverbank

It was Friday night. Things were tense in the Bailey household. They were all eagerly anticipating the arrival of babies. Mitzi's babies to be precise. Ten-year-old Jessica was worried about their lovely ginger cat as it was Mitzi's first litter, and she was worried that something might go wrong.

Supper was over and her parents were in the living room having cups of coffee. Jessica sipped her chocolate milk and watched their dog, Brandy, who lay fast asleep on the rug. She could tell he was dreaming because his ears and paws were twitching.

"I wonder what Brandy dreams about, Mum."

Her mum smiled at her. "He's probably just dreaming about his dinner or running through the fields on his walks."

"Maybe he dreams he's just about to catch a squirrel," said Jessica.

Her mum laughed, "Maybe so!"

Just then a tired and very pregnant Mitzi wandered into the kitchen. She went straight to her saucer for a drink of milk. Jessica could hear her lapping it up with funny little gurgling sounds until the saucer was quite empty. Then she wandered into the living room and meowed to attract Jessica's attention. Smiling lovingly, Jessica bent down to pick her up carefully and put Mitzi on her lap. The little cat purred and tucked her paws under her.

"You are so beautiful, Mitzi," murmured Jessica. "I can't wait to see your babies. I wonder will they be girls or boys? How long will it be now, Mum, before she has her kittens?"

"Anytime now, sweetheart. Tonight, or maybe tomorrow, or Sunday, even. They will come when they are good and ready."

Saturday morning arrived. While the family were all at breakfast, Mitzi roamed restlessly around the house, trying to find somewhere comfortable. She did not want to be cuddled, which was most unusual for her, and did not even want her milk or food. She meowed fretfully and roamed around the room.

"Why doesn't Mitzi rest, Mum?" Jessica asked, frowning with worry.

"It's natural, Jess," her mum told her. "She knows she is about to have her kittens and she's feeling restless. She'll be all right. She just wants to find a nice place to have her babies. Now don't you worry so much."

"She'll probably have them tonight," her dad added.

Tonight? Jessica hoped she could stay awake and watch, but in the end she couldn't help herself falling asleep.

Late that night, while the family were all sleeping soundly, Mitzi was making herself comfortable in Brandy's bed, patting down the cushion to make it just how she wanted. Then she lay on her side and waited.

When Jessica ran down the stairs next morning, she couldn't see Mitzi, but Brandy was still stretched out on the rug in the living room, snoring gently.

"Mitzi? Where are you!" she called as she searched the rooms for her.

Her parents came downstairs and went into the kitchen to prepare breakfast.

"Have you looked in Brandy's basket?" her dad said, giving his daughter a wink.

Jessica ran to look. "Oh! Oh! She's had them! Look, Mum, Dad! Four beautiful kittens! Oh, Mitzi – you are so clever! And we were all asleep and missed it all!"

"That's nature for you, Jess," said her dad with a smile.

"And she's just fine. See?" said her mum.

Fascinated, they watched Mitzi as she

roughly licked her little ones. They were so tiny, and their eyes were tightly shut.

"It will be a few days yet before their eyes open," said Mum.

As the kittens grew, Mitzi proved to be a fabulous mother, and Jessica was delighted to watch the kittens following Mitzi everywhere. In only a few weeks, they had grown to be adorable, mischievous little darlings.

Adorable to everyone, that is, but Brandy. He didn't mind Mitzi cuddling up to him, but he did object to her kittens. Each time they ventured playfully anywhere near him, he grumbled his displeasure, and barked at them if they took over his bed.

"Brandy!" Jessica would shout. "Dad, why is Brandy so horrid to the kittens?" she asked.

"I think he's probably a bit jealous of them, Jess. Don't forget you are giving the kittens a lot more attention than him."

"Oh." Jessica hadn't thought of that. She gave Brandy a hug. "I still love you, Brandy." Brandy gave her nose a lick and lifted a paw so she could scratch his chest.

"I don't think Brandy would harm them,"

added her mum. "But it wouldn't hurt to keep an eye on him with them."

Jessica had now chosen names for the kittens. There were three girls and one boy. All of them were ginger but with a white patch or two here and there. The first born, a girl, Jessica called Pinky because of her pink little nose. Number two, a boy, was Buttons because Mum said he was as cute as a button. Number three – the most mischievous of them all – was named Rascal because, well, the name suited her perfectly! Last of all was their youngest sister and she was called Darling, for she was indeed Jessica's very own little darling. Darling was the youngest and had a heart-shaped white patch between her eyes.

Day by day the kittens grew stronger and more adventurous. They would play outside in the garden, but only when someone was around to watch over them to keep them safe, for they had no sense of danger at all! They clambered and rolled, pounced and chased any small thing that moved.

Late one Sunday afternoon, the family, Mitzi, the kittens and Brandy shared a delicious picnic tea together outside in the garden. Afterwards, Mum, Dad and Jessica relaxed in their deck chairs, enjoying the warm, early evening sunshine, the sound of birds and the lulling rippling of the river as it flowed past the bottom of the garden. Beside them on the lawn, the kittens chased each other and Brandy dozed – or at least he tried to. The kittens seemed determined to plague him. Desperate to get some peace and quiet, Brandy finally jumped over the fence that guarded the riverbank, and lay down to snooze under a willow. He had learned that this was the only place he could get away from the pesky kittens.

It just so happened that Rascal and Darling had been exploring along the fence and had managed to squeeze themselves through a kitten-sized gap. The riverbank looked exciting, but they had no idea how dangerous it might be for them.

Suddenly, Brandy was rudely awakened by Mitzi's frantic meowing. Unable to squeeze under the fence herself, she watched helplessly as her kittens were sliding down the bank and

into the rushing water below!

Hearing Mitzi's cries, Jess looked up from the picnic and saw the cat at the fence with only two of the kittens. Immediately she knew what had happened.

"Mum, Dad, quick! The kittens are by the river, I think they've fallen in!" she screamed, tears already running down her cheeks.

Everyone ran to the fence and Dad jumped over, but he was too late.

Brandy had seen the kittens fall into the water and he had plunged into the river after them. He now had Rascal and Darling safely on the bank, where they shook themselves and mewed pitifully for their mother.

Dad rushed to the riverbank and picked

up the bedraggled kittens and brought them safely back. Mitzi immediately fussed over her two naughty children. Jessica took off her cardigan and wrapped up the shivering kittens, cuddling them both closely, while sitting on the grass close to Mitzi. Brandy, having shook himself thoroughly, jumped back over the fence and went over to Jessica. He flopped down next to her on the grass, stretching out with his nose on his front paws.

"Thank you so much, Brandy," whispered Jessica, "you're my hero!" Brandy lifted his head, flapped his tail and seemed to say, "It was nothing really."

Satisfied her two kittens were in safe hands, Mitzi lay down herself, and was soon joined by Pinky and Buttons. Before long, their two sisters, still looking a little damp, crawled out from Jessica's cardigan and crept sheepishly over to their mum. They all lay snuggled together, tired out from the adventure. And Brandy, the hero of the hour, didn't seem to mind when Rascal moved closer to his side. In fact, Brandy shifted a little to make the kitten more comfortable.

"Did you see that?" said Jess. "It looks as though Brandy won't mind the new additions to the family now, after all."

Seagull Strife

The ice cream wobbled on the end of the cone and fresh chocolate sauce dribbled over the child's podgy fingers.

"*Now!*" squawked Griff, the largest seagull. "All of us together. *Attack!*"

The ice cream didn't stand a chance. Ten seagulls swooped on the child. In a split second, wafer and topping had vanished – gobbled up by the feathered gang.

The child wailed, but the birds didn't notice. They had already spotted its parents.

"*Chips!*" Griff shouted again. "Get them while they're distracted with the squawking small one!"

"Great work, team," said Griff, landing on a bus shelter to finish his meal. The gang joined him, congratulating each other.

It was only Alfie, a younger gull, who didn't join in. He stayed on the ground behind the bench where the ice-cream-and-chips family were sitting. He'd been watching the human child – how it screamed with shock, how the tears trickled into its mouth. *Poor little human*, thought Alfie.

Over on the bus shelter, Griff burped. "What you doing down there, young Alfie?" he said. "You seen something else? Is it sandwiches? Ooh! What about pasties? I love a pasty!"

Alfie shook his head and flew up to the shelter, perching near the edge. He didn't want to get too close to his gang – they smelled of chips and he was so hungry. Instead, he slumped with his head in his wing. "I don't like stealing food," he said. "Didn't you see how upset the small human was? I feel sorry for it."

"Hahahaha!" The gulls threw their heads back. "Hahahaha!"

Griff laughed so hard, he choked a little on a chip. "Oh, that's a good one, Alfie!" he choked. "You're a funny youngster! Feel sorry for the human – good one!" And he started laughing again, setting everyone else off.

Alfie turned away. "It's not a joke. We shouldn't take food from people – from anyone

– it's stealing."

Griff stopped laughing and folded his wings. "Did you say 'stealing'?" He lowered his head and frowned. "Have you forgotten what we are, Alfie? We're gulls – Griff's Gulls – it's our job to steal. It's what we've always done!"

Alfie stared at his webbed feet. "But *why* do we have to?"

Griff and the other birds guffawed again, their bellies wobbling as they did. "You're hurting my ribs!" said one of the older gulls. "You're soooo funny, Alfie!"

"I'm not trying to be funny," said Alfie crossly. "We shouldn't upset people. Look at those birds over there." He pointed across the road towards the pier, where a family of holidaymakers was running in circles, trying to escape a mob of gulls. "See that? Greta's Gulls have stolen that family's doughnuts."

"Mmmmmm, doughnuts!" Griff's yellow eyes glinted. "Freshly baked, sugary doughnuts. Come on gang! Let's get over to the pier. Follow me!"

They swooped off, leaving a trail of squashed, feather-coated chips.

Seagull Strife

"Just because we've always done something," Alfie said to himself, "it doesn't mean we have to carry on doing it. We could change."

He watched as Griff and the gang hovered over a different doughnut family, circling the smallest human. To Alfie, it seemed to happen in slow motion: Griff spearing a doughnut with his sharp beak; the flap and fluster as humans tried to fend him off; the red, angry faces screeching at the birds. Alfie was too far away, but he could imagine the noise from the small human as its sweet treat disappeared inside a seagull. "I don't like hearing them cry," he said.

He stood up and stamped his feet. "I'm going to change things! We don't *have* to steal!" And he launched into the air, gliding across the busy town.

Alfie flew over the pier, ignoring the smell of burgers, fried onions, candyfloss and battered fish. "I don't need that sort of food," he said, although his mouth was watering. "Not all birds eat human food. I just have to look in the right places."

The pier and all its smells lay forgotten behind him. Alfie had reached the pebbly beach and the endless wide ocean beyond. *I'm a sea bird!* he thought, proudly. *I can find all I need down there in the ocean!*

Steering into the breeze, he landed on the beach. The wind seemed stronger here and he wobbled sideways, his feathers ruffled. "Right. I shall catch a fish – that's what we're meant to do!" And he marched towards the sea, tripping over a clump of seaweed.

By the time he reached the shallow waves, Alfie had so much seaweed caught round his legs he was quite worn out. "Ah, the water! That will get rid of this pesky seawe— *Oh!* It's freezing!" He yelped and flapped out of the waves. Slowly, he lowered himself back onto the water and peered into the grey sea, trying to spot a fish. But he could see nothing but thick, green, slimy seaweed.

"I can do this, I can do this," Alfie muttered, wading back and forth through the water. By now, his feet (still tangled in seaweed) were going numb and his bottom was particularly chilly, due to the constant bobbing of the

waves. "Stop splashing me!" he shouted to a wave. "Don't you ever stop?"

He turned away again, feeling silly. "Of course they don't stop, Alfie. This is nature. This is— Oh! A fish!" He sploshed backwards, ducking underwater, as he caught sight of a silvery fish. Excited, and swallowing mouthfuls of seawater, he struggled upright. "Where are you, little fishy?" he spluttered, peering into the gloom. "I know you're in there. You can't get away from me!"

Whoosh! Alfie stabbed at the fish with his powerful beak again and again.

No! He missed.

Urgh! He missed again.

Ouch! He hit a rock!

Coughing and spitting, Alfie splashed out of the water and flew to the safety of a small rock. *That didn't go very well, did it?* he thought, shaking water from his feathers. *Keep trying, Alfie. It will take practice. We all have to start somewhere.*

Alfie took a break. He watched some of the other birds diving into the sea and carefully studied what they did. After a while, he decided to have another go. This time he hovered above the water, gliding steadily, keeping his eyes peeled for fish. He noticed a whole shoal of tiny slivers, glistening under the waves. He folded his wings back and prepared to dive. "I've got you, you swishy treasures!"

This time, his beak missed the stone... but also the fish. They vanished immediately, scattering into the ocean.

"Come back! Let me eat you!" sobbed Alfie. "I'm so hungry!"

But the fish had gone and Alfie bobbed on the waves, too tired to fly anymore.

He made his way back up the beach. His tummy rumbled. He could hear the noise from the pier. Without even realising it, he had arrived underneath the huge platform on its massive metal girders. Music thumped above him, blending with the sound of people shouting and giggling and machines blaring. Adding to the din, a slow stream of smells wafted towards him. He stopped and lifted his beak. Chips, sausages, pizzas, pies... Oh, it was torture! Alfie closed his eyes. *Think of the small human. Remember its shriek as Griff stole its ice cream. You're not like those gulls, Alfie. You're better than that!*

He opened his eyes and stared at the rock pools underneath the pier. Rock pools! They were nature's doughnut stalls, weren't they?

Bursting with excitement at his new plan, Alfie hopped onto the nearest rock. His webbed feet hit shallow water – really shallow – and actually quite warm compared to the freezing ocean. "Now then, let me see." He swished his beak through the pool. Straight away, he spotted something scurrying through some seaweed. "A crab!" He dipped his face in the water. "A delicious sweet crab! Come to me, little sideways walker... *ouch!*" Alfie shrieked as the crab's pincer pinched a feather from his face. "That's not fair!" He rubbed his cheek. "But then I suppose I was going to eat you." He sighed and glanced at the other rock pools. What else could he eat?

"Ah ha!" Alfie's tummy groaned as he noticed the pale yellow shells clinging to the side of the rock. "Limpets!" he said. "Delicious, nutritious, healthy limpets!" He'd seen birds pulling these shells from rocks. It looked easy. Tottering across the uneven stones, he headed for the first shell, fastening his beak on the creature.

"*Nggggg!*" He heaved. He tugged. He clutched the shell with his feet, he flapped his wings wildly, groaning, heaving and straining, but nothing, nothing, *nothing* would budge that limpet.

"It's glued to the rock!" Alfie flopped on the ground. "It's a super-powered shellfish! How do those other birds get them off?"

As always, no one answered Alfie's questions.

Alfie plodded away from the rocks and rested on a patch of dry grass. Tears of frustration fell down his beak. "I'm so hungry," he wailed.

"I'll have to go back to the gang. I'll have to face everyone laughing at me!" He pictured the gulls, roaring and shouting. He stopped crying. "No! I won't let them know I've failed! I can't give up. I can't." But as the wind blew harder and the sky grew darker, Alfie wasn't sure what he was going to do.

Early next morning, Alfie was back underneath the great pier. He'd spent a terrible night huddled behind a pile of pebbles, cold, hungry and scared. He missed his noisy gang. He missed their warm feathers, their loud snores and even their messy eating habits. If only they weren't so mean. If only they could help him catch fish and limpets and crabs, then they could all live so happily. But even as the words formed in his head, Alfie couldn't help frowning. That greedy gang would never squelch through icy seawater looking for fish. There was too much free, easy food in the town where the humans lived. Why would they struggle on the cold beach and risk being nipped by an angry crab?

Just then, a large object fell onto the nearby shingle, making Alfie jump. He stared at the square package. He blinked. He sniffed. Something smelled wonderful. Something smelled truly, deliciously marvellous. Alfie waddled towards the package and saw a half-eaten pizza lying in its box. Just lying there! Not swimming away, not stuck to a rock, not armed with dangerous pincers and not stolen from anyone!

"Pizza!" breathed Alfie. "My favourite!" He fell on the crusty delight, gulping huge, cheesy mouthfuls and filling his poor empty stomach. "It has anchovies!" he cried. "I get to have fish after all!"

As he finished the last crumb, he looked up suddenly. "I haven't stolen this pizza, have I?" But the pier was deserted. Everything was OK. Relieved he hadn't upset anyone, he ran his beak over the pizza box, checking for any minute scraps. Finally satisfied, he heaved himself back to the pebble pile where he fell into a deep sleep.

When he woke, Alfie stretched and yawned, feeling so much better after his meal. But he'd had enough – enough of struggling on this wild, unfriendly, dangerous beach. It was time to go home – but not to steal!

With a full tummy, it took him a while to stagger back from the beach. By the time he arrived in the town, the pavement bustled with people eating all sorts of goodies. Alfie was so tired, he didn't have enough energy to fly and, added to that, he *still* had the seaweed wrapped round his feet. So he hobbled along the road, glancing in dustbins as he went past. *Look at all this food*, he thought. *Humans just throw it away*!

He stopped for a rest on one of the large, green dustbins and stared at a nearby bench where he could see a human taking a croissant from a white paper bag.

"Mmmmm!" Alfie watched the human sink its teeth into the pastry. "He's got jam on it – I love jam! I wonder if it's strawb—"

"*Oi!*" The human jerked its head up as a mob of seagulls attacked. "Get off!" it shouted, kicking out and waving its arms. But the seagulls flapped and shrieked, pecking at the paper bag.

Alfie shrunk back. It was Griff and the gang. Oh, how he missed them. But look! They were so awful. The poor human clung to its bag, but Griff was right there, ripping chunks out of it. Suddenly, the human dropped the bag and grabbed hold of Griff. The gang seemed to explode, squawking and scattering, flying off in all directions. Alfie watched in horror as the human clutched Griff by his neck. "I'll teach you to steal my breakfast!" it roared. "You horrible, greedy, thieving pest. I'm going to—"

Without thinking, Alfie slipped from the bin and lurched towards the human. Screeching and flapping, his beak wide open, he ran as fast as he could. The human looked up in surprise just as Alfie tripped over his seaweed covered feet and fell face first into the human's lap. "Hey!" it shouted.

Alfie panicked and flapped. His wings hit the human's nose. With another deafening yell, the human jumped up, letting go of Griff and losing the remains of the croissant in the process. "Get away from me!" it bellowed, running down the street. "Pesky birds!"

Griff and Alfie sat on the bench staring at each other. "You saved me!" said Griff.

"I did?" Alfie could hardly breathe. "I mean,

yes. I did!"

The other gulls started fluttering back, landing in a huddle around Alfie.

"Good to see you, Alfie!"

"Where've you been?"

"You just saved our Griff!"

Griff's feathers stood up like spikes. "No thanks to you guys!" He gave each bird a cold stare. "Where were you when I needed you? Scarpered, the lot of you! It's only Alfie here who could be bothered. Thanks, pal."

The gang rested on their bus shelter and

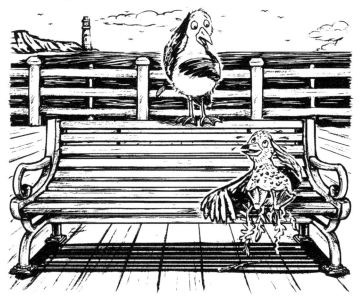

Griff untied the seaweed from around Alfie's feet, while Alfie told everyone about his time on the beach. Each gull roared with laughter as they listened to tales of fish and crabs and limpets, but somehow Alfie didn't mind. It was funny when you thought about it. He had been hopeless at living off the sea.

"We did miss you, young Alfie," said Griff, leaning back and gazing at the night sky. "And I'm glad you turned up when you did. You deserve a reward. What do you want?"

Alfie snuggled into the warmth of his gang. "Well… there is one thing…"

"Name it," said Griff. "Anything at all."

"I want us to stop stealing."

The birds gasped.

"But we have to steal!" said Griff. "You nearly starved to death out there. Couldn't even catch a measly little crab – you said so yourself!"

"I know!" Alfie fluffed his tail feathers. "I don't mean live off the beach, that's too hard now – I don't think any of us know how to do that anymore. I just mean we could take the food the humans don't want, that they've thrown away. You know… from the bins."

Griff blinked and thought for a while, staring at the other gulls.

"From the bins, eh?" He nodded gently. "I suppose we wouldn't have to fight the humans for their food anymore," Griff added, rubbing his neck.

"I had pizza this morning!" chirped Alfie. "With anchovies and everything! It was totally scrummy and no one even minded. In fact, I was helping, really, by keeping the beach tidy."

Griff chuckled. "Dear little Alfie, always so thoughtful, eh!" He slapped Alfie on the back. "It's a revolutionary idea, pal. You get your wish. From now on we, Griff's Gulls, will only eat food that is not wanted. Rejects. Throw-aways. Litter. That's our new food."

Alfie cawed with delight. "Thank you. You won't regret it!"

"You'd better be right," said Griff. "Now go and get me a croissant. I'm starving."

The Lonely Bullfrog

In a forest far away, beyond the highest mountains in the world, there was an old cabin made of logs hewn from the ancient trees around. It had been there a great many years and it smelled of earth and pines. It was the home of a very old woman named Edna Witherspoon, who had grown mean and bad-tempered over the years. The few neighbours she had were afraid of her. If they as much as passed by her cottage, she would shout at them, and threaten to place evil spells upon them. This being so, they all kept well away and warned their children never to go that way, either, for there were rumours that children had vanished, never to be seen again!

One day, Edna Witherspoon was out picking wild blueberries to make a pie when she heard a child crying. She searched all around her and eventually found a little boy in among some long grass and shrubbery. She was not pleased

to see him and wanted him to go away.

The little boy, Lucas, was lost, hungry and just wanted his mother.

Complaining bitterly, Edna took him into her cabin and gave him some special soup that she had concocted. It contained a spell that changed Lucas into a rather large bullfrog. Then she stamped on the ground next to him, to scare him away.

"Shoo, you little horror!" she shouted at him. Terrified, Lucas leaped away and hid under the nearest bush, shaking.

Later, when he thought Edna had forgotten about him, he went into the forest to explore and found a little stream where he could enjoy the things that bullfrogs enjoy. And he did for a time, but deep inside, Lucas the bullfrog knew that he was really a little boy. How was he ever to get back to his real self?

But old Edna Witherspoon, however, had not forgotten him. Not content with having turned Lucas into a bullfrog, she hunted him out each day, determined to make his life miserable. And each day, when she found him, she would pick him up and carry him back to her cabin, forcing poor Lucas to make the long journey of escape day after day.

"Go on!" Edna would shout as she placed him on the cabin floor. "Get out of here!" And with a dismal croak, each day Lucas would hop quickly away in a different direction, wondering where he could go to be free of Edna and her cruelty.

"I must get as far away from her as I can, and find my mother," he thought. "Maybe some of the other creatures in the forest will help me."

After a very long trek for a bullfrog, Lucas stopped to rest beside a river. He saw a fish jump out and snap at a fly. Maybe the fish would help him.

"Mr Fish," he called across. "Could you help me find my mother?"

"Go away and leave me alone," said the fish, crossly. "I have flies to catch. I don't have time to look for your mother."

"Sorry," said Lucas, upset by the cruel words of the fish. He plopped into the river and swam a little further.

It wasn't long before he stopped for another rest on the bank and saw a beautiful white swan gliding past. The swan was very handsome – and very arrogant. Desperately, Lucas called out to him, "Please, Mr Swan, would you help me find my mother?"

With a flourish the arrogant swan flapped his elegant wings.

"How *dare* you speak to *me* you ugly bullfrog? Be off, I say! Why should I want to help you? How careless of you to have lost your mother in the first place!"

Lucas felt awful. He hadn't meant to lose his mother.

Just then, another bullfrog swam past.

"Excuse me," said Lucas. "Could you help me find my mother?"

"What does she look like?" asked the bullfrog.

"I…" Lucas paused and a painful lump grew in his throat. "Why, I don't remember," he said with a cry.

The other bullfrog shook its head, "Can't remember what your mother looks like? Pah!" And it swam on, leaving Lucas alone once again.

"It's no good," he said to himself, licking away his tears with his long, bullfrog tongue. "I'll just have to manage on my own."

The Lonely Bullfrog

It was getting dark, so Lucas settled down on the riverbank among some soft, tufted grass and looked up at the starry night sky. Exhausted from all his travels, he fell into a deep sleep.

As he slept, he dreamed of a beautiful lady. She was crying. Lucas wondered why she was so sad. Maybe she had lost someone, too. He felt sorry for the lovely lady and cried with her, and she offered him comfort.

When Lucas woke up the next morning, he remembered his dream. It seemed so real. Something about it stirred a distant memory in his young mind. But what did it mean?

On he journeyed, not daring to stop for long, forever fearful that Edna Witherspoon would find him. And each night, he would dream the same dream of the sorrowful lady.

After many weeks of travelling, Lucas awoke one morning, his tummy crying out for breakfast. He was about to hop into the water to look for some food, when he heard a duck quack. He had long given up hope that anyone would help him, but he tried nonetheless.

"Excuse me," he called. "Would you please

help me to find my mother?"

But the duck just shook himself, showering Lucas with water. "I have no time for you today, bullfrog. Go away!"

"It's hopeless," thought Lucas as tears streamed down his cheeks. "No one wants to help me. No one cares!"

Just then, he sensed someone behind him.

A soft, kind voice said, "Oh! What a sad little bullfrog!"

He turned to see who was speaking and was amazed.

Standing there was the lovely lady of his dream. She smiled at him. He blinked. Was she real? He wanted to speak to her, but could only croak mournfully.

To his surprise, she picked him up and cradled him gently in her hands. Lucas immediately felt very safe. Her hands felt soft and smelled of flowers. Then, just like in his dream, she began to cry and as she did, her tears fell onto the little bullfrog.

Suddenly, his whole world began to spin and a wonderful sensation crept over Lucas. What was happening?

The lovely lady now held a little boy in her arms. Lucas was no longer a bullfrog! Astonished, she stared down at his face and gasped as she recognised her son, who had been lost to her in the forest all that time ago. She had been searching for him ever since.

"Lucas! My boy, Lucas. I've found you at last!" she cried with joy. "What happened to you? Where have you been?"

She hugged him close as if she would never let him go. She kissed his face again and again. Now a little boy once again, Lucas hugged her back. He remembered her! He knew he was safely held in the loving arms of his mother – the lady in his dreams. No more searching, no more running from dreadful Edna Witherspoon!

He told his mother everything that had happened.

"I remember being lost in the forest," he recalled. "The old lady who lives in the log cabin found me and took me home with her. She fed me some soup that turned me into a bullfrog. But now, being with you again, Mother, the spell has broken."

His mother hugged him tightly. "My poor, brave Lucas," she sobbed. "You are safe now. I shall never, ever lose you again!"

All this time, Edna Witherspoon had been hunting for the little bullfrog. She was furious he had escaped. She was afraid that, should his mother find him (unlikely as it seemed), her spell would be broken. And she couldn't have the boy telling people what she had done! Edna decided, therefore, to brew another potion for when she eventually found the wretched bullfrog again – a potioin that would make the transformation irreversible.

She put two pots on the stove and made another batch of her soup. In the pot on the left was the soup she would have for supper; in the pot on the right she added secret ingredients to make the cursed concoction.

Once they were cooked, Edna was about to pour herself a bowl of soup for her supper, but just as she lifted the ladle, there was a knock at her door.

Irritated at being disturbed, she flung open the door in a rage. "How dare you…" she began to shriek, but there was no one there.

She picked up her stick and went outside, looking left and right, shouting curses into the night, sure that she'd spot some pesky child playing a game. But she saw no one. Only the breeze knocking the tree branches against her cabin.

Muttering, Edna returned to her supper. She served herself a large helping of her delicious soup, and sat back at her table and began to eat hungrily.

Edna thought herself a clever woman, but she was no match for an angry mother.

Having returned Lucas home to the safety of his family, his mother had gone to the old log cabin in the forest and tapped at the door with a long branch. She had watched from the open window as Edna had gone to the door and, as the wretched old woman had shrieked warnings and curses at the wind, Lucas's mother had reached in through the open window and swapped the two pots. Left went right and right went left. Then she settled back, hidden among the trees, and watched.

Edna had barely swallowed the final spoonful of soup when she vanished!

The Lonely Bullfrog

Lucas's mother crept forwards and peered through the window once more. On the chair at the table, sat a fat, ugly, toad. Croaking with rage, it hopped onto the floor and crawled into the forest.

Lucas's mother returned home to her family and her beloved little boy, and they did indeed live happily ever after.

The other neighbours noticed that Edna Witherspoon had disappeared but no one looked for her – after all, their lives were much happier now the cruel old lady had gone. At that same time, a fat, ugly bullfrog, which seemed to hop angrily at travellers' feet, was spotted by many of them as they journeyed through the forest. But if anyone made the link between the missing woman and the ugly bullfrog, they didn't say a word!

The Magic Sprout

Flo's dinner looked delicious. Sausages, mashed potato, tasty carrots and peas. There was only one problem. Well, three actually – sprouts. Flo stared at the three horrible green balls and wondered how she was ever going to eat them.

"They look mouldy, she said, prodding a sprout with her fork. "And they smell like a compost heap."

Dad sighed, folding his arms across his apron. "You haven't even tried one! How do you know what they taste like?"

Flo put down her knife and fork. "You can tell from the way they look."

"That's not true," said Dad. "You have to try things!" He started wiping crumbs off the table. "I'd like you to eat one please, or there'll be no dessert." Flo knew Dad had made his special sticky toffee pudding.

Flo groaned. "But that's my favourite!"

The Magic Sprout

"Exactly." Dad opened the oven and sent a waft of caramel-sugary heat across the kitchen. "But you have to try a sprout first."

Flo gazed at the yummy pudding glowing in the oven and then back at the pale sprouts. "I don't think I can," she said. "They make me feel sick."

Dad closed the oven door. "Fine. No pudding then. I'll have mine in a minute with some ice cream." He wandered into the living room, leaving Flo alone.

She picked up her fork and poked one of the sprouts. Even that made her shudder. She dropped the fork and put her chin in her hands.

"Sprouts will make you super strong, you know."

The voice came out of nowhere, making her jump. "What?"

"Sprouts make you strong," said the voice again.

Flo whipped her head round, scanning the kitchen. "Who's there? Dad? Is that you?"

But Dad was chatting to Mum on the phone, his voice muffled in the living room.

"It's not your dad!" The voice was louder this time. "It's me. Look on your shoulder."

Goosebumps crept up Flo's arms. Slowly, she turned to her left.

"The other shoulder!"

Flo gulped and glanced to her right. "Oh!"

A plump, green fairy dressed in what looked to be sprout leaves, stood on Flo's shoulder beaming a wide smile. Her hair was green and tied in two tight balls on her head that looked just like sprouts! "Hello!" said the fairy. "Lovely to meet you."

"B-b-but..." Flo wobbled on her chair. "You're a...!"

The fairy hopped off her shoulder and waddled along her arm. "Fairy? Yes. But I'm not just *any* fairy," she said. "I'm the Fairy Guardian of the Highest Sproutiness, but you can call me Sprig – that's my name."

Flo could hardly believe it. "You're... *talking!*"

Sprig perched on the edge of Flo's plate and smiled, displaying a set of shiny green teeth. "Yes, I know it's a lot to take in, but just go with it for now. We haven't got long before your dad comes in." Sprig pointed to Flo's dinner. "All sprouts are delicious and nutritious and they'll make you big and strong." She paused, holding her finger over one of the sprouts. "But if you eat this one right here, you'll be double-triple-*quadruple* strong."

"Quadruple?" said Flo. "You mean like a superpower?"

Sprig nodded. "This one's extra special because I'm giving it some Sprouty Sprinkles." And suddenly Flo's plate was bathed in a glow of emerald lights that flickered and sparkled. There was a strange twinkly sound, like the high notes on a piano and Flo gasped. "That's the most amazing plate of food I've ever seen!"

Sprig fluffed her hair. "Yes I'm quite pleased with that one myself. Now come on – a mouthful of sprout – this beautiful one here!"

Flo didn't need telling twice. She leaned forwards and grabbed the sprout, taking a small bite. "It's not great," she said, swallowing. "But it's not as bad as I thought."

"Of course it's not bad!" Sprig jumped up and down on the table. "Try another one – mix it with some mashed potato! Oh, you're going to be so strong!"

Spurred on by Sprig's excitement, Flo scooped some potato onto the sprout. Within moments, a second whole sprout had disappeared. "Right!" Flo leaped to her feet. "Let's try out my powers."

"Flo?" It was Dad, calling from the living room. "Can you come here a minute? I've dropped my phone."

Flo ran in to find Dad peering behind the sofa. She marched forwards, grabbed the sofa and lifted it – clean off the floor!

"Hey!"shouted Dad. "Flo! What are you doing?"

Flo giggled, raising the sofa above her head.

The Magic Sprout

"There's your phone!"

Dad stood still, mouth open. Quickly, he knelt and retrieved his phone. "Now put the sofa down, Flo. You're going to hurt yourself."

Clomp! Flo put the sofa back in place.

"Goodness, Flo, you gave me a fright!"

"It's OK, Dad." Flo started looking around for other heavy things. "I ate a sprout – only it was magic and now I'm like Super Girl!" She whizzed into the kitchen and gobbled up a third sprout. "It worked, Sprig, it worked!"

Behind Flo's mug of water, Sprig smiled.

Still chewing the green vegetable, Flo rushed into the back garden where Grandad was working. "Hi, Grandad," she said running towards him. "Let me help you with that."

Grandad had been trying to dig a stubborn tree stump out of the earth, huffing and puffing and going red in the face. He put his spade down and laughed. "That's very kind Flo, but—"

Flo knelt in the mud and gripped the roots with two hands. There was a ripping, splitting noise and she wrenched the entire stump – along with its earthy roots – out of the ground. She hurled the stump sideways and dusted her hands off. "Amazing, isn't it? It's because I ate my sprouts!"

Grandad flopped down on the garden bench, wiping sweat from his forehead. "Sprouts?"

Flo began to lift anything she thought might be heavy – the stone birdbath, the lawnmower, the trampoline, the climbing frame and even the plastic sandpit full of sand! *"Wheee!"* She held each object above her head, before plonking it back on the grass. "This is so much fun!"

She was about to lift the garden bench –
with Grandad still sitting on it – when Dad
called Flo and Grandad inside. "Come and look
at this," he called.

There was a commotion outside on the
street. Dad opened the front door to see a
crowd of people gathered on the pavement.
They were standing next to a double-decker
bus, looking fed up. "Everything all right?"
asked Dad.

"Not really," said a man with bulging
shopping bags. "Our bus has broken down.
We've had to get off and wait for a new one."

Flo pushed past Dad. "Climb aboard
everyone!" she shouted, running to the bus.
"I'll get you home."

"No, hang on a minute." Dad shook his
head. "I don't think—"

"Jump on!" Flo tried to wave people on
board, but they stared at her as if she'd told
them to start flying. "I'll have to show you,
I guess." She ran along the pavement to the
back of the bus, rolled up her sleeves and
pushed as hard as she could. "One... two...
three...!"

With a loud rumbling noise, the wheels started to turn and the bus lurched into action. The people gasped and grabbed hold of each other, while the driver nearly dropped her flask of tea!

"What's going on?" she shouted.

"The lass is moving it!" said the man with the shopping. "Let's get on! She's going to take us home!"

There was a lot of murmuring and nudging, but one by one the passengers clambered up the steps and shuffled into their seats.

"Are we ready?" shouted Flo. "Off we go!"

Grandad stood next to Dad. "What on earth's going on today?"

Dad shrugged, speechless, as he watched the bus roll down the road – powered by his seven-year-old daughter. He gave himself a shake. "Wait a minute, Flo!" And he dashed after her. "I should help you – I've eaten my sprouts too!"

Much later, Flo and Dad returned from the bus stop, having dropped everyone off. The driver had thanked them as they pushed the bus back to the garage where it could be

The Magic Sprout

repaired. Back home, Dad went to get the sticky toffee pudding, which Grandad had rescued from the oven, while Flo looked around for Sprig.

"I did it!" she whispered, glancing at the kitchen table. "Sprig?"

The green-haired Sprout Guardian appeared from behind the mug once more, grinning and waving. "Told you!" she squeaked. "Super Sprouts!" and she promptly disappeared in a cloud of green haze.

Flo yawned and wandered into the living room where Grandad lay snoring on the sofa. She suddenly felt exhausted as well, and didn't think she'd be able to lift that sofa now. Perhaps she'd better have some more sprouts.

"Dad?" said Flo sleepily.

"Yes, poppet?"

"Can we have sprouts again tomorrow?"

"Again?" Dad frowned. "Er… maybe we'll try a different vegetable."

Flo smiled and snuggled into Dad's warm arms. *I wonder what power I'll get if I eat broccoli?* she thought.

Grandpa's Gloves

"Time to go to Grandpa's house," called Mum.

Kai groaned as he kicked the football. It flew straight over the net and just missed the kitchen window. Kai hated Sundays. Every week they spent a boring afternoon sitting in Grandpa's stuffy living room. It wasn't that he didn't love his grandpa, but it was just so tedious, sitting around with nothing to do. All Grandpa did was sit in his armchair and talk about the past.

At Grandpa's house, Kai sat in his usual place by the window while his mum and grandpa chatted together. He stared out at the back garden, wishing he could go out and have a kick about. It was school team try-outs next week and Kai needed to practise. He enjoyed football, but to say he wasn't very good was an understatement. He couldn't kick the ball straight to save his life, and whenever he tried to dribble with it, his feet tangled and he fell flat on his face. Even so, it didn't spoil his love of the game.

"Can I go out in the garden for a bit?" Kai asked.

"Oh, you don't want to go out there, lad. It's much too cold," said Grandpa. "Why don't you look in one of those photo albums? There's some pictures of me when I was your age."

"Maybe later, Grandpa," Kai replied with a sigh. He was never going to be good enough for the team if he didn't practise. He might as well give up now.

When the football try-outs came around, Kai stood nervously in line waiting for his turn at taking penalties. One by one the kids in front of him kicked the ball, swooshing it into the back of the net. Finally, it was Kai's turn. He stepped up to the ball. The net looked very far away. A big, older boy stood in goal, waiting. Kai took a short run up and kicked the ball as hard as he could. The ball flew through the air. He watched it, miserably, as it flew far wide of the goal post, missing by a mile. Kai trudged back over to the bench. He had no chance of making the team now.

Grandpa's Gloves

The next day, Kai checked the team list and, as he expected, his name wasn't up there. He wasn't even a substitute. He sighed. He'd just have to face facts: as much as he loved football, he was never going to be any good at it.

Kai stuck to playing football in his back garden, kicking the ball against the garage wall. And he began to feel relieved that he hadn't made the team. No matter how much he tried, he couldn't kick the ball straight, and the only thing he had managed to tackle was a tree when he had run straight into it, too busy looking at his feet as he dribbled! With his lack of skill, he would have made a complete fool of himself on the team, and ruined their chances of winning the championship. He was much better off just playing on his own where no one could see how bad he was.

However, at school a few weeks later, Coach Matthews ran up to Kai in a bit of a fluster.

"Kai, are you still interested in playing for the school football team?" he asked.

"Well…" Kai hesitated.

"Great." Coach Matthews didn't wait for a reply. "Our goalie has broken his arm. He's going to be out of action for a while. So we'll see you at the match next week. Thanks, Kai!"

And he rushed off again before Kai could say another word. Kai was speechless.

After school, his mum was waiting for him with a huge grin on her face.

"Good news about the football team, isn't it?" she said. "I've already signed the permission slip."

Kai managed a weak smile at his mum, but inside his stomach was in knots. The next match was the final. The trophy match!

That weekend, Kai went to his grandpa's as usual. All he could think about was the upcoming football match. He had never been a goalie before, but he was sure he would be just as bad at it as he was in every other position.

Grandpa looked at Kai sitting miserably by the window. He was even quieter than usual.

"What's wrong, Kai?" he asked. "Is something bothering you?"

"No," replied Kai. "It's nothing, Grandpa." His grandpa wouldn't understand. Football probably wasn't even invented when he was a kid!

"Your mum tells me you've made the school football team. All that practising must have paid off," Grandpa smiled. Kai said nothing. "I'll have to come and watch one of your matches."

"Oh, you don't have to do that," Kai said glumly. "There's no point anyway."

"Why ever not?" asked Grandpa.

"Because I'm useless. I can't play football. I can't kick the ball straight, I can't score a goal, and I bet I'll be rubbish as a goalie, too. So unless you can magically make me an amazing player, I won't be on the team for long," Kai blurted out, bitterly. "It's only, until the real goalie's arm heals."

Grandpa looked at Kai thoughtfully for a

moment. But then Kai's mum came back in with tea and the subject was dropped.

He was dreading the upcoming match. Kai couldn't even practise being a goalie without someone to kick a ball at him. His mum tried, but she was even worse than he was!

Kai got home from school one day surprised to find his grandpa sitting on their sofa.

"Your mum had to go out, so I thought I'd come over," said Grandpa. "Are you ready?"

"Ready for what?" Kai asked.

"For football practice!" Grandpa said, getting up from the sofa. Kai had never seen him move so fast. He then saw that his grandpa wasn't wearing his usual comfy trousers and slippers. He was wearing a tracksuit and trainers. Kai tried to hide a giggle. How was his elderly grandpa going to help him train for the football match?

"Thanks, Grandpa, but you don't have to," said Kai.

"*Have* to? I *want* to. Come on, let's get started!" He headed out to the back garden and Kai followed him. "Let's warm up with a little kick about, shall we?"

Grandpa's Gloves

Kai picked up the ball. He would have to take it easy on his grandpa – he didn't want to hurt him. He kicked the ball gently and it rolled slowly towards his grandpa. To Kai's surprise, Grandpa kicked the ball up and started bouncing it expertly on his knee. He then kicked it hard towards Kai's goal and it shot straight into the back of the net.

"Wow!" said Kai, his mouth hanging open in surprise.

"Surprised your old grandpa knows how to play, eh? Bet you thought they hadn't even invented football when I was young, didn't you?" Grandpa said with a twinkle in his eye. Kai felt his cheeks burn. "Now, let's get down to some training. We've got work to do!"

Kai and his grandpa had a great time playing football. Kai had never seen Grandpa so active, or so happy. Grandpa taught Kai some great tricks and gave him tips on how to control the ball. Kai was definitely much better than when they had started.

They went inside for a break and Kai spotted a large box on the table.

"What's in here?" he asked, peering inside.

It looked like it was full of tatty old books.

"Ah," said Grandpa, grabbing a book from the box and flipping it open. Inside were old pictures and newspaper clippings of a football team. Kai immediately spotted a familiar face in the lineup. It looked just like him. It was his grandpa and, by the looks of it, he had been a really good footballer when he was younger. His team had won lots of competitions.

"Wow," said Kai, flicking through the pictures. "You were really good. What position did you play?"

"I was the goalie," Grandpa said, and Kai looked at him in disbelief. His grandpa was a goalie, just like Kai was about to be.

Grandpa went to fetch them each a glass of squash while Kai pulled out some trophies from the box. They were big and shiny, and they had Grandpa's name engraved on them. Kai wished he could win a trophy like this.

While they had their drinks, Grandpa told Kai some tricks to tell which way people were going to shoot, and Kai listened eagerly.

They went back outside, and Kai practised being in goal. Kai wasn't nearly as bad as he thought he would be. He was pretty good at catching, and he enjoyed all the jumping and diving. And, using the tricks Grandpa had taught him, he even managed to stop some of Grandpa's strikes going in.

Kai could tell that his grandpa was getting tired, so they decided to stop for the day. He was already feeling much better now about the upcoming match.

Grandpa took the box over to the sofa, and while Kai read some more of the newspaper clippings about Grandpa and his team,

Grandpa rooted through the box, looking for something.

"I knew they were in here somewhere," said Grandpa, pulling out what he had been looking for. Grandpa held in his hands an old pair of grubby white gloves. Kai looked at them, confused. "These are my lucky goalkeeping gloves. I wore these for every match I ever won. I want you to have them."

Kai tried them on. They were a bit big, but when Grandpa tightened the wrists, they fit much better. The leather was soft and worn where Grandpa had used them to save countless goals, and Kai could almost feel the excitement that Grandpa would have felt when wearing the gloves out on the pitch. Maybe with Grandpa's lucky gloves he would actually have a chance at winning a trophy too!

"Thanks, Grandpa," said Kai, giving him a big hug. "Will you come to the match on Saturday?"

"I wouldn't miss it for the world."

When Saturday came around, Kai woke up early. He couldn't wait to get out on the pitch. He only hoped he'd be as good in a real match as he had been in his garden with his grandpa.

Grandpa came over early to see how Kai was and to give him a last-minute pep talk.

"Don't forget, even the best goalies can't save every goal. If one gets past you, don't let it get you down. Focus on the rest of the game."

Kai nodded, concentrating hard on everything his grandpa had to say, and then they all went off to the match together.

Kai slipped on his grandpa's gloves and felt the energy run through him. He could do this, he was sure of it. As he walked out onto the pitch, he passed the trophy that was waiting to be presented to the winning team. It was only a little one, nowhere near as big and shiny as some of the ones Grandpa had, but Kai felt excited. He imagined holding it up high above his head at the end of the match, standing proudly with his team.

Kai took his place in goal. It was a lot scarier on a big football pitch than in his little back garden, and a lot harder to keep track of the ball with so many people running around passing it backwards and forwards. Kai felt a little overwhelmed, and when the first shot at the goal came, he hadn't even seen it coming. It had flown straight past his head and into the back of the net. Everyone groaned as the other team celebrated their first goal. Kai felt terrible. They had only been playing for a few minutes and he had already let his team down. Kai spotted his mum and grandpa in the crowd. They gave him a thumbs-up, and Grandpa waved at him encouragingly. Kai took a deep breath as he threw the ball back into play.

Kai's team played really well, and the ball didn't come near him again for the rest of the first half. Finally, the whistle blew for half-time and everyone walked off the pitch to get a drink. Kai was sure his team were going to have a go at him missing that save, but everyone was really kind and encouraging, patting him on the back and telling him not to worry. Kai began to feel a bit better. Grandpa came over to see him.

"Sorry, Grandpa. I should have saved that. I should have been paying attention," Kai said.

"Don't let it get you down. It's your first

time. Remember, even the best goalies can't save every goal," Grandpa said. "Now you go back out there and remember what we practised."

The whistle went and Kai walked back onto the pitch for the second-half feeling slightly better. He tightened his grandpa's gloves on his wrists and squinted up the pitch, concentrating hard on the ball, not letting it out of his sight as it bounced around and shot through a tangle of feet. Before he knew it, the ball had flown from one end of the pitch to the other and was suddenly hurtling straight towards him. Kai took a deep breath and threw his arms up. He caught the ball expertly in his gloves and the crowd went wild. Someone from his team ran up and hugged him. Kai could barely believe what he had done – he had saved his first goal! Kai grinned, clutching the ball proudly. Until he realised that the match was still going on, and everyone was waiting for him to throw the ball back. Kai passed to one of his teammates, and before long the ball was at the other end of the pitch and their team had scored a goal. It was one-all! Kai jumped and cheered with the crowd.

The game continued, and both teams tried harder than ever to score another goal. The ball kept flying at Kai, but each time, somehow, Kai found himself catching or knocking the ball safely away from the goal, to the cheers of the crowd and the rest of the team. Kai felt great. Grandpa's gloves were working perfectly. It was so much easier to catch the ball with them on, and all of his grandpa's tips were really helping, too.

The final whistle went, and the two teams were still tied one-all.

"It's going to be a penalty shoot-out to decide who will win and get the trophy," Coach Matthews told the team as they huddled together. "You know what that means, Kai? It'll just be you against their team's best strikers. But don't worry. Just do your best."

Everyone slapped Kai encouragingly on the back as he walked nervously towards the goal. A member of the other team stepped up to the ball. Kai watched him closely, looking for any signs as to which way he was going to shoot. There! Kai noticed the slight glance at the top right corner of the goal. He jumped to the right and his hand knocked the ball away. He had saved it! Then it was his team's turn. Save! Kai groaned. The next player from the other team walked up to the ball. Again, Kai watched him closely as he flinched to the left. Kai dived left but the ball was wide anyway and flew way past the goal post. Then Kai's team scored the next penalty. They were in the lead! Kai just had to save the next goal and they would have won.

Kai watched, but the player was hard to read. Was that a glance to the left? A flinch to the right? The boy took a short run-up and Kai chose to dive left. The ball flew straight past him, right down the centre of the goal. He had missed it. Kai felt sick. Had he just blown their chances of winning? Luckily, Kai's team scored their next penalty. They were still in with a chance. It all depended on Kai. He watched as the next striker seemed to look left, but Kai had a feeling he was bluffing. The boy paused. Kai had to choose, and quickly. In a split second Kai made his decision and jumped right. The ball flew straight at him and he

caught it. Save! He had done it! His team had won the match!

The team rushed towards Kai, cheering and jumping around. They were presented with the trophy and everyone got a chance to hold it. When it was passed to Kai, he held it up high above his head, surrounded by his ecstatic team, grinning from ear to ear. He saw his mum and Grandpa cheering in the crowd, and Kai beamed with pride. It was a thousand times better than he had imagined.

After the presentation, Kai's grandpa came over and gave him a hug.

"I knew you could do it," he told Kai proudly. "You know, I think you might be better than I ever was!"

Kai glowed.

"I couldn't have done it without you, Grandpa," Kai said. "And your lucky gloves."

Then Coach Matthews came over.

"This is my grandpa," Kai told Coach Matthews proudly. "He was a top goalie when he was my age."

"That must be where you get your talent from," Coach Matthews said, shaking

Grandpa's hand. "I don't suppose you want to help me get this team into shape, do you? We're looking for a volunteer assistant coach, and I think with your help we could go all the way to the national championships."

Grandpa looked at Kai, and Kai grinned up at him hopefully.

"I'd love to," Grandpa said.

Now Sundays are Kai's favourite day. They don't go around to Grandpa's house anymore. Instead, Grandpa collects Kai and they go to football practice together. Grandpa is a great volunteer coach, and Kai is the best goalkeeper the team has ever had. They haven't lost a match, and Kai never plays a match without wearing Grandpa's gloves.